HARD TACKLE

WORTH THE WEIGHT BOOK TWO

JASON COLLINS

ACKNOWLEDGMENTS

A very special thank you to:

My cover designer, Cate Ashwood Designs.

My editor, Tanja Ongkiehong.

My proofreaders, Leonie Duncan and Shelley Chastagner.

Cover photographer Eric McKinney of 6:12 Photography.

CONTENTS

TYLER

ANOTHER SATISFYING DAY OF WORK AT THE SHOP WAS BEHIND ME, another drink to unwind at The Chisel was ahead of me, and another cloudless, starry night sky was above me as I drove down the country roads through the one and only Winchester, South Carolina. I watched my headlights push through the light fog that was settling in after sunset as my 1970 Chevy Chevelle, my pride and joy, tore down the road. On nights like this, I wished I was back in high school so I could hit the field for a quick pickup game of football with the guys and end the day with strong, athletic bodies crashing together and a little stress relief on the side.

For the reality of tonight, I satisfied myself with the roar of my engine instead of a ball in my hands. I couldn't exactly call myself a mechanic if I didn't take pride in my car, could I? The rumble I felt through the wheel under my firm grip reminded me how much care I had put into this gem of a muscle car over the years. Considering I'd just spent another full day working on cars that weren't always taken care of properly, I knew it was time well spent.

But all that hard work left me with a different kind of tension to work out, and that was the one area that Winchester wasn't quite as good at providing. Besides, even if there were gorgeous men around, the truth was that I hadn't felt completely confident in my appearance since gaining some weight. Still, on nights like this, I liked heading to The Chisel to grab a quick drink, but I knew I wouldn't find any handsome men with strong hands, ready to take me back to their place to work out all that stress with a roll in bedsheets that smelled like pine and the fresh outdoors.

Just that thought made the shaft between my legs thicken, and I rolled my shoulders back in my seat as I turned into the gravel parking lot of The Chisel. But as I did, my heart skipped a beat at the sight of the vehicle I saw parked in the lot.

Like mine, it was vintage, but this one was a truck: a 1968 Ford F-100, painted blacker than the night sky and, by the looks of it, kept in just as loving condition as my own ride. I'd recognize that truck anywhere not just because of its beauty but also because of its owner: Mason Glass, the personal trainer from the gym. If that truck was here, that meant he was here, and that made my heart beat faster.

I parked my car and hopped out, gravel crunching under my work shoes as I headed for the front door. I stopped in my tracks as the door swung open, and I was caught off guard when Mason stepped outside.

Our eyes met, and my mouth fell open at the sight of him. He was wearing a tight black T-shirt that showed off every one of those rippling muscles he spent so long perfecting, and his jeans hugged his body just as tightly. If only he were entering the bar instead of leaving.

"Hey there," Mason said with that boyish, charming grin that somehow only a former quarterback could pull off with that much finesse. "We're ships passing in the night again, aren't we?"

"Gotta leave The Chisel in good hands until I get here," I joked back at him, bumping arms before we passed each other.

Mason and I saw each other once or twice in front of The Chisel, enough that we traded a familiar smile and a nod, but it was rare that we were there at the same time.

He headed toward his truck, and despite myself, I couldn't keep from looking over my shoulder to glance at that ass of his. It was just as round and taut as ever in those tight jeans, and it made my cheeks warm up as I tore my eyes away.

Even though we played together on the football team in high school, our lives barely intersected anymore. He got busy with his career and his own life after graduation, I had assumed, so while we did see each other once or twice in passing, fifteen years was a hell of a long time. He probably didn't even remember my name. We had different circles after high school, plain and simple. If I had my way, things would be a little different. As Mason turned his key in the ignition, I noticed that his truck sounded a little off. I thought about asking him if there was something wrong, but I was too absorbed in thought to speak. I found myself drifting into a fantasy about what I'd do with him.

If I could, I'd head over to his truck and pull him out of it. I'd slip my hands around his waist and into the back pockets guarding that tight ass of his, then walk him backward to press him against his truck. The smell of the seats and the metal would fill my nostrils as I'd press a kiss to his neck and push my hips against him. He'd feel just how hard I was for him, but more interestingly, I'd feel his cock through that thick denim.

My body would melt as he'd hug me close to him and tilt his head back, letting my teeth caress the sensitive skin under his perfect jawline, and I'd smell his cologne as I tasted him. He'd put his hands around my face and bring my lips to his, and sparks would fly between us. Piece by piece, I'd strip the clothes off my body until I was nude before him. I'd look up at him, hands on the roof of the truck as he glared at me with that hungry, predatory smile at the door of the car before hopping inside and wrapping his arms around me to catch up after all these long, lonely years...

I snapped out of my daydreaming at the sound of laughter coming from the open doorway. I stepped inside and felt the warmth of The Chisel surround me, and I heard snippets of conversation that sounded just as warm and inviting. I looked out at the road one last time, wondering if Mason's truck was giving him trouble, but it seemed to drive off just fine, so I chuckled and headed inside.

The Chisel was Winchester's only bar, and like many businesses in town, its name was an homage to the town's biggest export: woodworking. There must have been more woodworkers and carpenters in Winchester than anywhere in the tri-county area, and we were damn proud of our work. Of course, I never came anywhere close to touching wood in my line of work. That was a shame, really, but crafting beautiful tables and bed frames didn't exactly make for a well-rounded economy.

The bar was filled with the usual people, and a few of them nodded to me at the sight of my familiar big frame. I had always been a guy who took up some space, but I had to admit, I'd put on a little extra over the past few years. That was another thing that made Winchester special, as far as I was concerned: we had the best food around, hands down. Southern cooking was something you could smell about a mile before you even hit the town sign.

Most of the people who hung out here knew each other. There were no strangers in Winchester, after all. That kept the conversation in the bar going strong because if there was one thing small-town people down here in the Carolinas liked to do, it was gossip.

"You're late," the bartender, Parker, said with a grin as I approached the bar and sat down on an empty stool.

"You know damn well we're backed up." I chuckled. "Just got around to working on your cousin's El Camino. How the hell do you let him drive around in that thing?"

"We're only related by blood," Parker said with a smirk. "Gettin' the usual?"

"Yessir," I said, rolling my shoulders back. "I'll have some nachos, too."

"Predinner snack?" Parker asked as he took out a glass and started pouring me a pint from the tap. "Or is it a 'nachos for dinner' kind of day?"

"Just you watch, I can do worse than nachos if I put my mind to it," I said with a wink.

"Oh lord, don't," Parker said with a laugh. "I don't want you keeling over on me anytime soon."

Parker and I were just joking around, of course. That was how we got along down here. But I had to admit there was some truth to what he said. I hadn't exactly been eating healthy, if such a thing was even a concept most Winchester folk could grasp, besides maybe Carter Foster and that backyard garden of his. Me, I satisfied myself with nachos right after work and some fried chicken before bed, and on my days off, it was pretty damn tempting to just order a pizza and make the delivery person the first one I talked to that day.

I was a hard worker with a hell of a lot of muscle under the weight I'd put on. I sure didn't mind indulging myself now and then, and there was nothing wrong with that.

Within a matter of minutes, I had a frosty beer in my hands, and I felt that familiar sense of comfort wash over my body as I took the first sip. I wasn't a heavy drinker by any standard, but sometimes a cold glass of beer was the perfect cure for post-work weariness. As I drank and glanced up at the soap opera playing on the television above the bar, I raised an eyebrow. Onscreen was a dark-haired man about my age, sauntering into a woman's bedroom wearing a winning smile and not much else. I caught Parker's eye and gestured vaguely toward the TV.

"That the same guy who was killed off last season?" I asked, squinting up at the handsome actor. I heard Parker sigh.

"Yeah," he groaned. "Adrian Bannister, the prodigal son of the wealthiest family in a small town in upstate New York. They made it seem like he was poisoned in an insurance scam at the last season finale, but he's back. He's played by Jesse Blackwell."

I nodded slowly, impressed. "Wow. You sure know a lot about it."

"My wife is obsessed with Bannister Heights. She's been watchin' it for years. And Adrian's her favorite character. I thought once they killed off his character in the show, I might not have to hear about it anymore, but now they've gone and brought him back from the dead. That Jesse Blackwell is too popular right now for the showrunners to let him go that easily."

He chuckled good-naturedly.

"Fair enough. I can see why your wife likes him," I remarked.

5

"Hey, whose side are you on?" Parker teased.

"Your wife's. Always." I laughed.

Parker shook his head, still grinning, and stalked off to help another customer. I sat for a moment, just watching the drama unfold on the TV above my head. Then, through the din, I heard familiar voices talking at the booths around the bar, and my ears pricked.

"I hear even Tommy Dawson is flying in from Madison to make it," said Bill Walsh, who was sitting next to his wife on one side and a row of his friends on the left, including Jared McInnes.

Those two had been thick as thieves back in the day, and from what I could tell, they still were.

"No shit?" Jared laughed. "Wonder what he's got going on these days. Remember that time he dinged Principal Jackson's car and blamed it on Carl? Hoo, you should have seen the shade of purple Carl's face turned when he found out."

A roar of laughter came from the table, and I smiled to myself. I knew exactly what they were talking about without having to ask. It was all anyone was talking about the past week, it seemed, and that wasn't surprising for a small town like Winchester.

The Winchester High School Reunion was coming up. Fifteen years ago, I had thrown my square cap up into the air along with all the classmates I'd grown up with, and from that day forward, we were all free. High school had some good memories for me, and most of those good memories were on the football field, which was true for a lot of the guys who hung out in The Chisel these days. Including the door guy, Marshall, who I noticed was already eyeing the group with some concern from his position by the entrance. The atmosphere at The Chisel was usually too friendly for bar brawls to be much of a worry, but if a fight ever did break out, Marshall was the hulking wall of muscle kept nearby to put a stop to it. He was always a good guy back when we played football together, a real team player, even though he was known to get a little aggressive on defense, and he was in charge of keeping the peace now, too. Funny how that worked out.

"Ain't too many of us who left Winchester in the first place," said

Leah, Bill's wife. "Can't imagine many people will be missing. Might as well have it here at The Chisel."

"Right?" Bill laughed. "Not like we got any celebrities coming out of Winchester."

"I dunno about that," said Hunter Kincaid, the high school football coach, who was sitting at the far end of the bar with Mark Sullivan and the latter's boyfriend, Carter. "We've got Winchester's star mechanic right here, don't we?"

I couldn't keep a smile off my face because I knew Hunter was talking about me. I turned my head and nodded to acknowledge the compliment, but Bill scoffed, rolling his eyes.

"Now, a real local celebrity we need to get an RSVP from is the one who just walked out of here," Bill said.

"Mason Glass was one hell of a quarterback," Jared admitted begrudgingly, smiling. "Weren't you on the team when he took us to state?"

"The glory days," Bill said, sighing. "I've never seen an arm like that man has. It's like he was born to do this. You know he got that college scholarship, right? That boy could've gone places and retired back here by now to do all that fancy gym shit he's got going on now."

I had to chuckle to myself as I listened. Small-town politics amounted to football scoreboards a lot of the time, for better or for worse. I was happy with my time doing that, but I never considered myself hung up on the past. Missed opportunities, maybe, but I only looked back on those days with what I thought was a healthy amount of fondness.

"I don't know. He's pretty damn *good* at that fancy gym shit," I heard Mark murmur to Carter, and the two of them exchanged a knowing smile.

Mark didn't get along with Bill and Jared, and it was no surprise. The latter two were assholes, if you asked me, plain and simple. They had been football players along with the rest of us back then, but they were jackasses even then, regardless of how good they had been. Mark had never been an athlete like Carter, Mason, or Marshall, but he was good people.

"Come to think of it, I think the whole team from our class is going to make it," Rhett Anderson spoke up, looking around at the group. "Why the hell aren't we having a reunion game?"

Everyone in the bar who was paying attention to the conversation, which was just about everyone except Parker, was silent for a moment as we all looked at each other. Marshall and I exchanged expressions of curiosity. I could tell he realized what a potentially charged suggestion Rhett had just made, and he was poised to step in if the tension got too high.

"That's... a good question!" Hunter said with a growing smile on his face as he turned to look around at the rest of us. "Hell, our star quarterback just left the bar, and the best linebacker Winchester has ever seen is sitting right there!"

He was referring to me, and he happened to do so just as Parker set down my plate of nachos in front of me. Golden cheese was oozing over the hot, flaky chips, and all the fixins from jalapeño slices to black olives and chunks of ground beef were melting down the cheese as the savory aroma hit me.

"I'm game," I said without missing a beat, turning around to put my hands on my knees and smile around at the crowd with much more confidence than I felt deep down. "If most of the team is going to be here, we just split them up evenly and get anyone else who wants to play involved. Not like we weren't all playing the game from the day we could hold the ball, right?"

A general cheer went up around the room, and I grinned down the bar at Hunter, who looked like he was over the moon at the idea of a friendly reunion game. I glanced back toward the door, and Marshall gave me a stoic shrug, which was pretty much a high five coming from him. And I had to admit, the idea didn't sound half-bad to me, either. I had been planning to show up and show off my car, but I'd like to smell the fresh-cut grass on the field again.

"Yeah," Jared said, grinning at me, "judging from those nachos, I reckon you might not be quite as 'spry' as you used to be, but don't worry, we'll go easy on y'all," he said as he patted his stomach.

I caught on to his meaning, and I raised my eyebrows, glancing down at my gut. Sure, maybe I had put on a few pounds in the last few years, but it hadn't really crossed my mind as a problem. But the way Jared said it and the way he high-fived Bill a moment later, it all didn't sit very well with me.

"Oh, yeah? I remember a certain someone losing his lunch after that tackle you took from Preston Whittaker before you even played your first game," I said, taking a fierce bite out of a beef-loaded nacho.

"Tell yourself whatever makes you feel better while you enjoy that bar food, big guy." Bill laughed. "If you wanna put your reputation where your mouth is, then I think this game ought to happen."

"Agreed," Hunter said, nodding to me to let me know he was on my side. "I'll spread the word. We've got a little over a month till the big day, right?"

"Yessir," Carter said, now leaning back against the bar and sizing up everyone at Bill and Jared's table. "More than enough time to get ready, if you ask me."

"Then it's settled," Jared said, slapping his hand on the table and nodding to Bill. "The high school reunion game is happening. Winning team gets a round of drinks here at The Chisel, courtesy of the losing team."

A cheer went up through the bar, and I looked over to the other guys at the bar, who exchanged a solemn nod with me. I cracked my knuckles and tossed back the rest of my beer, but in truth, I wasn't quite as sure about this as I was letting on.

Yeah, I had been a damn good linebacker. And I sure as hell hadn't been lying when I said I was down to put my reputation on the line against some of my classmates and teammates. But as the bar continued chattering about what was soon to be the latest buzz in Winchester's thriving gossip mill, I couldn't help but think about that comment about what shape I was in.

If it were all about brute strength, that would be one thing. I had forearms so thick most people couldn't get their hands around them, and I had always been a big guy, my whole life. But I couldn't deny that my diet hadn't been the healthiest in the world the past few years. It wasn't something you thought about in your early thirties, like I was, when you had a full day of work ahead of you all the time.

But I wasn't about to let anyone down. I'd meet them on the playing field, and then we'd see who ate their words. And though I'd never breathe a word of it to anyone at this bar, there was one more thing that tugged at the back of my mind about the prospect of playing again.

I'd get to hit the field with Mason again.

And *that* was a chance I wasn't about to pass up for the world.

MASON

I was staring out the back window at my beloved 1968 F-100, which was hitched up and rolling with quiet dignity behind the tow truck. The evening country sounds of the outdoors and the beautiful tapestry of starry sky above me were usually relaxing, but tonight were anything but that. The sun had already slipped down to the horizon, and the occasional streetlight was only bolstered by the eerie glow of the moon, making it difficult for me to see what was going on back there. That truck was my baby, and I was still having trouble wrapping my head around the fact that she might be in serious trouble.

"Rotten luck, huh?" grumbled the tow truck driver behind the wheel beside me.

"What?" I said, distracted. "Oh. Yeah. Real bad luck. I still don't understand what happened there. She was powering along just fine, and then... well, she wasn't."

"It's the moon," the tow driver said sagely.

I turned and frowned at him in confusion. "Excuse me?" I asked.

"The full moon. Weird stuff happens this time of month, plain and simple. Ask anyone who works in a hospital or the police department. They'll tell you the same thing." He chuckled.

I gazed at the side of his stubbly face for a moment, unsure if he was joking. But then it dawned on me that he might well be serious, and I brushed it off. I wasn't about to debate the moon with the guy responsible for getting my truck to the garage in one piece. I sat quietly, listening to the muted crooning of the country music station playing in the tow cab, trying not to let my concern get out of hand. *Just wait and see what the mechanic says*, I told myself.

It didn't take too much longer before we were pulling into the lot behind the garage, surrounded by the glistening metal grills and hoods of cars in varying stages of disrepair. The tow truck rolled to a stop under the flickering neon sign that read PEARSON AUTOMO-TIVE. I popped open the side door and jumped out, looking around for someone to help us. The tow truck guy sure was taking his sweet time getting out of the cab, and I squinted impatiently into the shadowy garage until my eyes landed on something much more attractive than the gleaming vintage cars and trucks gathered in the lot. My heart skipped a beat or two as my eyes adjusted to the low light and the guy in my view came into focus.

It was Tyler, an old teammate from high school football I never got the chance to ask out, and he was gorgeous. I had just seen him outside The Chisel yesterday and was happy to see him again. Tall and broad-shouldered, with a chest the size of a wine barrel and thick arms that looked like they would suit a lumberjack or a weightlifter. He was dressed in a plain, coarse white T-shirt tucked loosely into his jeans, as well as heavy black work boots. There was a filthy-looking rag slung over his right shoulder, and there were oil stains down his front. At his feet sat a gigantic toolbox, and there wasn't a doubt in my mind that the former linebacker knew how to use each one of those tools with perfect precision. He had his short, dark hair slicked back out of his face, and there was a smudge of oil or grime across his left cheek that made him look as though he had just stepped clear out of the pages of some bawdy men's magazine or maybe a specialty calen-dar. I wondered which month he would be. July, maybe? He was certainly hot enough to represent the hottest month.

As I watched him bend over the popped-open hood of an old

Corvette, my worries regarding my truck went scampering away into the dark recesses of my mind, replaced by steamy thoughts of what the mechanic's body looked like underneath those filthy clothes. I was a pretty tall guy, and given that I worked at the local gym as a personal trainer and fitness instructor, I certainly was no lightweight. But Tyler, with his roguish good looks and linebacker build, had me absolutely mesmerized. I couldn't help but imagine him slowly looking up from the hood of the 'Vette, those piercing dark eyes falling on me. I licked my lips imagining the way that brawny dreamboat might furrow heavy brows at me, his mouth opening to ask me a question.

What kind of man had he become over the years? Would he be the kind of guy who was overly patient and gentle? The kind who would ask if it was okay to kiss me? Even though he was a big guy, something about him made me feel like I could take control and boss him around. I could see him going along with whatever I said, following my instructions. Admittedly, I was a take-charge kind of man myself, and the idea of having this handsome giant at my beck and call made me hot around the collar. I felt my body heating up, a bead of sweat rolling down my spine as I pictured pinning that fine mechanic into the wall of the garage, rutting against that solid trunk of a body.

My heart thumped like crazy when I thought about the days when he was one my old teammates, when I had cheered him on from the bench when he was playing defense. The memories came back in swift succession: the sensation of fuzzy, bright white lights illuminating the green turf as our stocky herd of footballers had huddled together for one last pep talk. It had been near the end of the game, our home team caught in a perfect tie with the rival team from across the lake. I could still hear the hoarse chanting of the cheerleaders, their pom-poms glittering like tinsel. I could feel the bass beat and hear the brassy fanfare of the marching band perched in the bleachers behind us. Some days, after practice, I had liked to sit at the very top, where I could see the entire field as well as the miles of mostly untouched forest that stretched out beyond the high school campus. I could remember the numbers on the backs of our jerseys as we sprinted down the field.

I had joined the football team for two reasons. First of all, because nearly everyone had attended the games as a sort of town-wide, cultural bonding activity. In a rural region like ours, there hadn't been a whole lot else to do, quite honestly. In the Southern countryside, football reigned supreme over all else. And second of all, because even back in high school before I had fully realized my sexuality, I had enjoyed watching my fellow football players dart up and down the field in those tight white pants. I had loved seeing strong, powerful bodies push themselves to the limit, working through all kinds of stress and pain and adrenaline to carry our team to glory. Every high school game had been clouded in a thick atmosphere of highly contagious excitement. People had gone all out for these games, and we players ourselves had been essentially teenage royalty.

And now here he was, hunched over a Corvette with a wrench in one hand and a grimy, greasy rag in the other, and I was utterly entranced. That is, until my reverie was rudely interrupted by someone clearing his throat. I blinked rapidly and turned toward the sound to see a different mechanic, dressed almost identically to the hot one but wearing it with considerably less sex appeal. He was middle-aged and balding, with a sour look on his face. He was standing with his greasy hands on his hips, looking at me expectantly.

"Hello? You alive in there?" he said coarsely.

I nodded, biting back down my brief impulse to be curt with him. I reminded myself that my gorgeous, beloved truck's life was at stake, and I needed to stay on positive terms with the mechanic in charge of potentially saving her life. So, I forced a smile and stuck out my hand for him to shake, which he did a little reluctantly. I tried not to blanch at how clammy and oily his palm felt against mine.

"Sorry. I must have zoned out. It's been a long day," I apologized.

"You got that right," he groused. "It's nearly nine o'clock. We close at nine."

"I definitely did not plan for my truck to break down at this hour, but it is what it is," I told him, trying my damnedest to keep my annoyance in check.

The guy folded his arms over his chest and squinted at me. "All right. So. Tell me what happened," he prompted me.

"Well, I was driving home. I've noticed that she—my truck—has had a little cough when startin' up here and there lately but nothin' too concerning. When the weather gets chilly, she tends to get a little ornery. Happens every year, and with the hard freeze we got earlier last week, I just figured that was it. But then tonight she started chugging and puffin' out little poufs of smoke from under the hood as I was driving home on the back roads. I've never seen her do that before. It really scared me, to be honest," I explained. "Her carriage felt a little rough, and I got worried, so I pulled over to the side of the road and called the tow truck, just in case it's something serious."

"Mm. Yeah, that was a smart move on your part," the mechanic agreed. "Those back roads can be a little dicey if your vehicle's on the fritz. You been in any fender benders lately? Any bumps or scrapes?"

"No, sir. I'm a careful driver," I told him truthfully. "That truck is my pride and joy. I'd sooner jump off a cliff than let anybody tap her bumper."

"Well, that's sweet, but clearly something has gone wrong here, and I need to figure out what it is before I can diagnose your baby," he replied. "Unfortunately, it's gettin' near closing time as I said, and I've got a lot of paperwork to sort through, so looks like you're gonna have to wait until tomorrow morning for a diagnostic, all right?"

My stomach flip-flopped, and I took a nervous step forward.

"Wait. Can I convince you to just take a quick look before you close up for the night? I know I'm asking a lot of you, but my truck is very important to me. She's my most prized possession," I rambled.

The mechanic rolled his eyes and sighed. "Look, man. I'm gonna be straight up with you for a minute. That truck is old as hell. What year is it, sixty-nine?" he asked.

"Sixty-eight," I answered quietly.

"Exactly. That truck is only a few years younger than I am, and my body ain't exactly in fightin' condition these days either," he remarked.

I frowned, feeling my heart pounding yet again.

"What are you saying?" I pressed him.

15

"I'm sayin' there might not be much we can do for her," the mechanic admitted. "Just like people don't get to live forever, your truck ain't exactly immortal, either. No matter how much you might love it. These things have a lifespan, and once they hit the end of it— wham, they just die on you. Can't fight the passin' of time, my friend."

"But you haven't even looked at her yet. How can you know she's done for?" I pushed.

"Because I've been in this business for a long, long time, kid, and I know what the hell I'm talkin' about. That's how!" he retorted a little defensively.

"Hey man, can I go?" the tow truck driver asked from somewhere behind me.

I swiveled around and said, "Can you hold on just a minute? I might need a ride back home if I have to leave my car here."

The tow truck driver glanced at his wristwatch and groaned impatiently.

"Oh, you'll definitely need a ride home," the mechanic said with a snort. "You sure as hell won't be drivin' your truck anytime soon."

"Can you tack some overtime on the invoice? I just want some idea of what I'm working with here," I urged him.

He rolled his eyes theatrically and held up both hands in mock surrender. "All right, all right, already. Jeez Louise! I'll take a peek, okay? Just take a chill pill, man," he mumbled as he strode past me to my truck, which the tow driver was busy detaching from his own truck.

I fought the urge to go hover over the mechanic's shoulder as he popped the hood and took a peek inside. I could hear him faintly clucking his tongue and saw him shake his head a few times, looking extremely pessimistic. Meanwhile, I noticed with a jolt that Tyler had stopped working on the Corvette and was now quietly watching the scene unfold from his place in the garage. I wanted desperately to talk to him, to ask him for help. Something about his face indicated compassion. Patience. He looked like the kind of guy you could count on.

"Well, I was right," the older mechanic said, snapping my attention back to him.

I turned around to see him dusting off his hands on his shirt, giving my truck a very dour look.

I walked over with my heart pounding away painfully.

"Right about what?" I prompted, terrified of the answer.

"About how screwed this truck is," he replied with a shrug. "It's probably your transmission. Maybe even the engine. Doesn't look good, kid."

"How much?" I asked firmly, gritting my teeth.

He tilted his head to one side confusedly. "How much... what?"

"How much will it cost to fix her up again? Five hundred? A thousand?" I guessed.

He snorted. "Pfft. You think I'd make a big deal out of somethin' a thousand bucks could fix? Hell no. Buddy, the truck is ruined. You'd be better off buyin' a new one than sinkin' any more cash into this money pit," he advised.

"She's not a money pit," I protested fiercely. "Not to me."

"Hey, I just call it like I see it, man. The kind of repairs you'd need to make... it'd be like givin' a guy a whole body transplant," he explained.

"Then do that. Switch it all out. Special-order the parts. I'll... I'll set up a payment plan. I'll put it on my credit card," I offered, reaching into my back pocket to pull out my wallet.

But the mechanic just held up his hands, shaking his head. "I can't take your money and say it'll all work out. Unless you're some kind of undercover high roller with thousands in cash on hand, it just ain't gonna happen. I'm tellin' you, man. Just cut your losses and buy yourself a new truck. I have a pal over at the used car lot off Adams Road. I'm sure I can talk him into cuttin' you a good deal on an F-150 or somethin'," he said.

"I don't want a new truck. I *need* this one," I said stubbornly. "She means a lot to me, all right? I don't want to get into it right now, but it's got sentimental value."

"Come on, man. I don't know how else to explain it to you. I get

17

that you don't wanna let 'er go, but I'm tryin' to give you some good advice here. The truck is dead. Move the hell on. And now, if you don't mind, I have to start closin' up shop here. I got a family to get home to," the middle-aged mechanic snipped, blowing right past me.

"Can I please go now?" the tow truck driver asked.

I whirled around and sighed. "Yes. Fine. You can go. I guess I'll... I'll get a cab."

"Great. Have a good night," he replied and promptly climbed back into his truck and drove away.

I followed after the mechanic, still determined to get something done tonight. My parents had always told me I was too stubborn for my own good, and maybe that was true, but I wasn't about to give up on my beloved truck without a fight.

Just as I opened my mouth to say more, a new voice interrupted me.

"I'll look at it."

We both turned, startled, to see Tyler sauntering over to us. He looked at me intently, those dark eyes unreadable and yet... warm.

"What?" I asked softly.

"I said I'll give it a look in the morning," he said. "Maybe there's somethin' to be done about it. I could at least give it a try."

"That would be amazing," I said, lighting up.

The older mechanic waved his hand at us both dismissively and went into the small office, slamming the door behind him. Tyler offered a hand for me to shake, which I obliged gladly.

"Sorry 'bout Chet. He's kind of a hothead, and he gets grumpy in the evenings," he said. "My name's Tyler, in case you don't remember. Tyler Pearson."

I glanced up at the neon sign, then back at him. He smiled and nodded.

"Yeah. That Pearson, but my dad's still the owner," Tyler explained.

"Of course I remember your name. Wouldn't forget the team middle linebacker," I said, not mentioning that his role was only a fraction of why I remembered Tyler.

"Goes without saying for a quarterback like the one and only

Mason Glass, right?" Tyler said with an infectious smile. My heart fluttered.

"Yeah. And you were a linebacker. I passed you yesterday outside of The Chisel," I replied.

"That's right." He chuckled, "I'm the guy who seems to keep showing up when you're leaving. I usually played Mike back in the day."

'Mike' was football slang for the guy who played middle linebacker, one of the more tactical roles on a squad.

"Anyway, I can tell you really give a damn about that truck. She's a beauty. You must take real good care of her, huh?"

I nodded. "Yeah. She's my baby. First big thing I ever bought for myself years ago. I know it probably sounds shallow, but she's important to me," I elaborated.

"Doesn't sound shallow at all," Tyler replied. "Listen, if you're really gung-ho about gettin' her back on the road, I'll take her on as a personal project."

"Wait. Really?" I asked breathlessly.

He grinned warmly. "Yeah, of course. I can't guarantee anything, and we're backed up as hell, but I'll give it my best shot. And we'll find a way to work out the payment. It won't be cheap, but there might be some hope for her still."

"You're a godsend," I gushed.

His cheeks burned a ruddy pink that made him all the more endearing.

"Anyway, you still need a ride home. Wanna hitch a ride with me?" he offered.

Still a little dazed by this turn of events, I could only give a firm nod. I followed Tyler to his car, a beautifully restored Chevelle, and slipped inside, wondering what realm of heaven this angel descended from.

TYLER

WHAT IN THE HELL WAS I DOING? I WAS GOING OUT ON A LIMB IS WHAT I was doing, but realizing that wasn't about to stop me. I'd had to keep it cool when Mason showed up at my shop with that beauty of a truck, both because of Mason himself and his truck, but giving him a ride wasn't a turn I'd thought tonight would take.

Not that I was complaining.

The clean country air blew through the car as I drove with the windows cracked, and I had to keep resisting the urge to let my eyes drift over to him as we drove away from the shop. He was stunning. He sat in the passenger's seat with his legs spread and one large hand resting on the roof through the window, and the way he was reclining and letting his glassy eyes look ahead of him, he looked like a Greek statue in repose. There was something so powerful and peaceful about his body that made my heart pound, and I couldn't help but admire the little details about him like that. I wasn't trying to pay special attention; he just gave off that kind of powerful energy.

"I've got to say," Mason spoke up at last, "for the age of this thing, it's a pretty damn smooth ride. You must have put a lot of work into her."

"Oh, I have." I chuckled, feeling a blossom of pride in my heart. "I don't mean to say my work is my life, but the skills sure are. I've been working on cars since I was old enough to pop a hood on my own. It was just the kind of thing I couldn't resist."

"That's the thing, isn't it?" Mason said, grinning over at me. "You see these fierce, roaring engines blazing down the highway through town, and you know there's just this whole science and art form working together under the hood."

"If you're anglin' for a job at the shop, you're doing a pretty good job," I teased, but I was only exaggerating a little.

It wasn't that uncommon for people in Winchester to be more hands-on with their cars than most people would expect, but it was another thing entirely for someone to understand on a gut level why I loved spending time bent over an engine. And frankly, the way Mason put it with such vivid imagery like that had my blood running hot, and I had to fight to keep the smile on my face from being broader.

This was just a casual ride home, after all, not a lift to a date.

"I figured that 'Vette I saw you working on was yours," he said. "But if this is you, then I've seen you around town more than I thought."

"That Corvette's nice, but no, this is my baby," I said, patting the dashboard. "Fished her out of the scrapyard and restored it myself. If you thought the guys were a handful tonight, you should have seen the looks on their faces when I hauled this thing into the shop in the state I found her in. They said I was wasting my time, but I didn't even see it as wasted time, even at the times when I was worried it was hopeless. Turns out, a little patience and elbow grease goes a long way."

"You sound like you've got both in spades," Mason said thoughtfully, giving me a searching look that made me feel exposed, as if he was evaluating me with that piercing gaze.

"I don't know about that." I chuckled modestly, rubbing the back of my neck. "But I've got a reputation now. When you're elbow deep in cars as much as I am, 'lost cause' sounds pretty damn tempting as a challenge, no matter what the car is."

A pause fell between us, but it wasn't an uncomfortable silence. I knew exactly what was on Mason's mind before he even opened his mouth to speak.

"So I know you didn't really get a chance to take a look at the truck, but the other guy back there didn't give me the most hopeful prognosis. Is that a habit of his, or...?" He trailed off, tilting his head.

I thought carefully for a few moments about how best to word this without throwing Chet under the bus. He was rough around the edges, but like everyone I worked with, he was an alright guy, deep down.

"Don't mind Chet too much," I said. "He's always in a hurry to get out the door when it comes around time to close up shop, so more likely than anything, he wasn't giving it the look it deserved. That, and Chet likes to lowball people's expectations. He thinks it covers our asses in case a job looks easier than it actually is because nobody likes giving bad news when a customer isn't expecting it."

"That's not the worst way of doing things, sometimes," Mason admitted with a reluctant nod. "Better than getting disappointed down the road."

"I usually handle as much of the mechanical side of things as I can," I explained. "Everyone who works for me is qualified, of course, and I'd trust them with anyone's car, but it's still just a job for most people at the end of the day. I wouldn't blame anyone for that, 'course, but most of the time, I just try to keep Chet's expertise to the front desk."

I didn't like bragging, and even though the other mechanics tended to defer to me as the authority on anything that was outside their routine, I felt like it would be doing their hard work an injustice to come out and say that a vintage piece of living art like Mason's truck should have come to me first. In fact, I felt a little blush on my cheeks as I skirted around the subject like I did, but that only seemed to make Mason's smile grow.

"I hear you," he said. "Sounds like you've got a firm grip on things at the garage. Are you the sole owner?"

Did he just ask if I was single? No, no, you're reading into things too much, Tyler.

"No, my dad's still the name on the sign." I chuckled. "Not for much longer, though. He's working on retiring. 'Working' being the operative word there," I added.

"I mean, if there's one job that would be tough to retire from, it would be yours," Mason agreed. "And if he raised you, he must have a good head on his shoulders for it."

My blush grew, and I had to fight to push out of my mind the idea that Mason Glass might be flirting with me right now. He was probably just grateful I had agreed to work on a truck that one of my guys had called a lost cause. I shouldn't go reading into it too much. Right?

"Take a right up here. I'm on the far edge of town," Mason said, pointing to a turnoff that I took. "It's not exactly around the corner. Thanks again for this, by the way. I know it's a pain in the ass to take a new truck in right before closing as it is, so I wasn't expecting anyone to do so much as give me a ride."

"Winchester boys take care of each other." I chuckled, hoping my tone didn't give away my other reasons for wanting to jump in the car with Mason.

Of course, I would have given anyone a ride if they were stranded at my garage. That was just the manners I had been raised with, plain and simple. But the fact that it was a guy who I couldn't tear my eyes off was icing on the cake.

"Ain't it the truth." Mason laughed, laying on the local accent a little thicker than it might have come to him naturally. "But speaking of, are you going to make that high school reunion the whole town's talking about?"

As he brought that up, we happened to be driving by the high school itself. The dull glow of the sign was almost the same as it had been fifteen years ago, except for a few cleanings here and there. And just beyond it, the dark stadium lights loomed over it all, looking as majestic as they were hauntingly beautiful in the light of the full moon.

"Funny you should mention that," I said, glancing over at him to try to gauge his demeanor about the question. "I bet it's hard not to get reminded about it if the place is on your morning commute."

"You're right about that." He chuckled. "But hey, that's small towns for you. I hear about it at work, too. People like to shoot the breeze at the gym between workouts all the time, so I hear my share of it."

"So you've probably heard about the game that everyone wants to get together?" I ventured, still trying to probe for his reaction.

To my surprise, Mason gave me a puzzled look and blinked at me perplexedly, so I explained.

"Well, I suppose news travels fast, but not *that* fast," I said with a laugh. "Last night at The Chisel, some of the guys got to talking about who all was coming back into town for the reunion, and since you had just left and I had just come in, they got to talking about football on top of that."

"That tracks, I think I remember who all was in there last night," Mason mused.

"Right." I nodded. "So you know how they talk. Next thing I know, everyone's going down memory lane and deciding they want to get a football game together for the big day."

"Is that so?" Mason asked, smiling and scratching his jaw thoughtfully. "Huh. You know, that hadn't even crossed my mind. Funny how time changes you, isn't it?" he said, grinning at me. "Don't tell anyone the quarterback hasn't been thinking about football. It's been ages since I've even held a ball. But now that you mention it, I can think of a few familiar faces I wouldn't mind crashing into again."

"Yeah, when you put it that way." I laughed, feeling my heart racing at the thought of Mason's body colliding with mine somewhere besides the field. "See, if you work at the gym, you've got that advantage: you know who's working out and who isn't, and for the ones who *are* staying in shape, you know where their weak points are."

Mason laughed, nodding.

"Shoot, you're taking me back," he said, shaking his head. "I've never really been the type to look back on high school football like it was the highlight of my life or anything, but damn, it could be a rush sometimes. Out there on the field, the smell of fresh earth and tense air in your nose, adrenaline making you see things in the heat of the moment you'd never notice normally... from a trainer's perspective, football is kind of a blessing and a curse. I hate seeing people hurt themselves out there, but it shows how incredible the human body can be."

Just like how he talked about cars, the way he talked about the human body in the rush of a game made me wonder just how expressive a soul he could be, more so than I had been expecting by a long shot. I had to keep from smiling at the thought of a former star athlete waxing poetic like that, in a good way.

"Well, when you put it *that* way." I chuckled, "I gotta admit it sounds pretty appealing."

Mason looked mildly surprised at me, but there was still that thoughtful, almost playful smile on his face. Damn, he was a hard person to read, and it made me want to keep probing his mind for more.

"Were you thinking about passing on it?" he asked. "Nothing at all wrong with that, of course, but the more I think back, the more I'm pretty sure I remember you being a damn good football player."

"I did my job out there," I admitted with a nod, and that was about as much as I was willing to brag about myself. "It just hasn't been on my mind for... well, years, like you said. Not all of us work in a gym, so it's a little harder to keep the football body, if you know what I mean," I added, glancing down at my figure.

I would never have admitted it outright, but the comments I'd heard back in the bar last night had stuck with me through the day. I wasn't completely out of shape, of course, nobody could say that. I was a blue-collar worker, and that meant I could handle myself with just about anything life threw at me. But handling myself was one thing, and competing against a bunch of other guys in a full-contact sport was another thing entirely.

"Come on, I bet you had better times than that," he urged me playfully, nudging me with his elbow and grinning. "That feeling when you shut down a play so fast the offense barely has time to figure out what happened? That rush when you know you just powered through a block and hear a quarterback's helmet clatter when he hits the ground?"

"Quarterbacks like you?" I teased, letting a grin show itself despite my best efforts.

"Hell, I'll be the first to admit I'm speaking from experience on the other side of the fence." He chuckled. "I took so many hard tackles that I figure it must have been *some* kinda rush, right?"

We both laughed at that, and I found that his good cheer was pretty infectious.

"Yeah, tackling you would be something to remember," I said. "You look like you go down nice and hard."

"Careful now. Keep talking like that, and I'll want you on the other team so you can put your money where your mouth is," he said with a challenging grin.

I couldn't keep the blush off my face, but it was dark enough that I figured I was safe from being seen like that.

"Full-contact side of things aside," Mason said, putting his hands behind his head as he leaned back. "A mechanic's mind is a good thing out there. A team needs people with analytical minds like that."

"All right, if you'll be out there, maybe I'll see if I can squeeze into a uniform," I finally admitted with a grin that faded after a moment. "Just promise you'll wheel me off the field when all the junk food I've been packing away catches up to me."

"You look great to me," Mason said in a tone that made my heart skip a beat.

Mason had just said he was a personal trainer. There was no way he thought my body was anything to shout about... right? I didn't mind my looks, but I knew I wasn't a gym type by any stretch of the imagination.

"Take a left here, and my driveway is the first one on the right," Mason said quickly before I had a chance to open my mouth and try to formulate a response.

I was actually grateful for that.

"Well, life just gets in the way," I said vaguely, apparently so vaguely that Mason furrowed his brow. "Just don't expect me to be doing anything fancy. I'd have to change a lot to be the kind of guy I was back in high school."

We pulled up to a lovely little canary-yellow house with a large yard, and I had to admit it looked picturesque, especially thanks to the brick walkway leading up to the black front door. I looked to Mason with a smile, and I was surprised to see him looking at me very thoughtfully as a different kind of smile crossed his lips.

"How about this," he said. "I think I've got an idea. Do you have dinner plans? If you hear me out, I'll cook you up something good."

My eyebrows shot up, and I was frozen for a moment. Dinner with Mason to keep catching up? Damn, that was hard to turn down. Impossible, one might say.

"I'm free." I chuckled, turning the ignition off. "Sure, why not?"

What the hell am I getting myself into?

MASON

"You've got a great looking house there," Tyler remarked. "Love the brick."

"Thanks, man," I replied brightly.

It was nice to hear someone genuinely appreciate the work I put into making my home look inviting. Out here, people were less concerned with aesthetics than with practicality, but I could never resist a good project. My house was old, like my car, but I poured my heart and soul into preserving it as best I could. The old-fashioned wrought iron fencing that came to a gate at the mouth of the brick walkway was one area that showed the home's true age.

It was now peeling and rusty in spots, but I was a bit of a history buff, especially when it came to local architecture, so I couldn't bring myself to replace it. Besides, it wasn't like I ever left the gate locked or anything anyway. Here in Winchester, I never felt for even one second like my home might be under threat of invasion or attack. That kind of thing just flat out didn't happen here. Maybe once every few years some hooligan teenager would toilet-paper a house over Halloween, but that was pretty much where the police ticker ended. This was a community of families who never locked their doors, who never worried about letting their kids skateboard and ride bikes all over town. Everybody looked out for one another, and I trusted my neighbors the way one might trust a good friend. So my iron gate was more of an aesthetic choice than a practical one.

"Well, I think it's gorgeous," Tyler remarked.

I smiled softly, a blush of pride warming my cheeks. "Thank you. I've put a lot of work into it myself, and I've got a friend—you might know him—Carter Foster. He's a contractor and a damn good one at that, so I sometimes pick his brain for advice. I don't own the place yet, but I'm working on it. Right now it's just a rental, but the landlord is an old buddy of my mom's, so he's helping me start the paperwork to buy the place," I elaborated.

I couldn't help but feel another swell of pride at the genuine awe on Tyler's face. He shook his head and let out a low whistle as he drove us down the driveway along the side of the house. He glanced across at me with eyebrows arched.

"Damn, man. You're makin' me look bad by comparison," he said with a chuckle.

I waved my hand as though to dismiss his self-deprecation. "Nah. Everybody moves at their own pace. Some people immediately move out to another city. Some people stick around town but get their own place. Some people choose to wait longer. It's all good. We're human beings, not racehorses. We're not in competition," I told him, trying not to let my tone wander too close to motivational speaker territory, as was my reflex.

My job as a personal trainer meant long hours of essentially just hyper focused cheerleading and motivation. I loved it, of course, and found it to be an incredibly rewarding line of work. However, it did make it difficult for me to unplug from that way of speaking and interacting with the world. When you spent most of your waking hours doing everything within reason to motivate people and eat, drink, and breathe optimism, it was a little hard to turn that off at the end of the day. But luckily Tyler didn't seem at all fazed by my peppy platitudes. In fact, judging by the way he was gazing at me in the low, glowy light of the porch lamp, he was actually pretty intrigued. My heart did some kind of acrobatic backflip or something within my chest, and I had to remind myself to breathe and act naturally. Even though I was about to invite this gorgeous angel from another life into my home.

"So," I began casually, "you should come in for a drink. I've got ice cold beer in the fridge, plus I can make you a mean plate of brinner."

"Brinner?" he repeated dubiously.

I laughed and nodded. "Breakfast for dinner. Don't knock it till you've tried it."

"I'll never pass up an opportunity for breakfast food," Tyler replied brightly.

"Then let's go," I prompted, unbuckling my seat belt and stepping out of the sleek muscle car. I stretched as I walked up the side steps to the rickety wraparound porch, realizing it had been one hell of a long day.

Normally, by this point in the evening, I would have been too exhausted to even think straight, much less want to cook a full dinner and entertain a guest. But Tyler was different. Something about him energized me and pumped me up rather than drained my energy. He was intoxicating to be around, and I found myself looking for any way to keep him near me. What kind of magic did this guy have over me?

Tyler got out of the car and followed me up onto the porch to the front door. Not even bothering with the keys, I simply opened my unlocked door and walked inside, sighing with pleasure at the wave of cozy warmth inside. I unwrapped my scarf from around my neck and draped it on the coat rack by the door along with my pullover sweater, then kicked off my boots. Tyler looked vaguely stiff and uncomfortable at first, but then quickly followed suit. I was entranced by his every little movement, the way he whipped off his hat and hung it up, the way he gingerly untied his shoes and nudged them neatly into the corner behind the rack—he was just adorable, however way you sliced it.

"So, what's your beer of choice? You like lagers, pale ales, stouts," I listed off as I sauntered into the kitchen.

"Whatever you've got is fine by me," Tyler said, trailing behind me.

"Easy to please, just how I like 'em," I joked.

I gave him a wink and pulled a couple bottles out of the fridge along with some icy cold pint glasses. I gestured for Tyler to take a seat at the little bar on the other side of the kitchen counter and placed the beer on the bar. He pulled up a bar stool and watched me intently as I dug in the fridge again and took out ingredients for breakfast.

"So this breakfast for dinner thing... what do you have in mind?" he asked.

I grinned. "You sound hungry," I remarked.

"Always," he joked.

"Well, the plan is to make sweet potato hash. So what I'm going to do first is peel and dice a couple of large sweet potatoes," I explained, brandishing the potato peeler as I spoke. "I'm going to roast them in the oven for about thirty minutes at four hundred, flipping them over halfway through. While they're roasting, I'm going to chop up some garlic, onion, tomato, mushrooms, and collard greens."

"Damn. I'm intrigued," he said, eyes wide.

"But that's not all," I added cheerily. I loved talking about food and cooking. It was one of my biggest joys in life. "I'm going to fry up some turkey bacon in a big skillet, then drain some of the fat and sauté the vegetables in the remaining oil plus a small glug of olive oil to collect those salty little bits at the bottom. When the potatoes are done, I'll tip them into the skillet along with the veggies, then fry us up a couple of eggs. I'll top it all off with some fresh-chopped parsley and a drizzle of hot sauce, if you're so inclined."

"Oh, I most definitely am," Tyler replied enthusiastically. "Can I help somehow?"

"Well, considering you gave me a ride home, you've already done me the biggest favor of all, but if you'd rather keep your hands busy, I won't turn down help," I said. "Here, you can peel and dice the potatoes while I wash and chop the other veggies."

"Perfect," he said with a bright smile.

As we got to work on dinner prep, I asked conversationally, "So you work with your dad at the garage?"

He nodded, looking a little starry-eyed. "Right. He's been runnin' that place since before I was born. It's been his lifelong project. It's a real joy and honor to get to work alongside him, even if he doesn't do a whole lot of actual manual labor these days. He's got a bad back," he explained. "In fact, he's supposed to be retiring this year."

"Oh, really? That's awesome, man," I remarked as I began chopping a sweet yellow onion. I reminded myself inwardly to breathe through my mouth and not my nose, as that trick made it far less likely that I would tear up while handling a cut onion.

"Yeah, the problem is he's been sayin' he was going to retire for about five years now and it still hasn't happened yet," Tyler chuckled fondly. "That man would work himself to death if he didn't have me and Mom to slow him down."

"Are you going to stay on at the shop once he finally does retire?" I asked,

Tyler nodded. "Definitely. Dad says he'll only feel safe retiring if I'm the one left in charge. He's a friendly guy, but I guess he doesn't trust some of the other mechanics. At least, not as much as he trusts me," he mused aloud.

"Sounds like you three have a great relationship," I pointed out.

He was beaming as he peeled the sweet potatoes. "We do. I'm very grateful for that. Although we all get along and I worry about them so much it's made it very difficult for me to imagine moving out. I keep thinkin' if I move out, who will be there to take care of Mom if she falls in the garden or injures herself cooking?" He sighed.

"Well, if your dad retires, surely he'll be around to look after her," I said.

"That's true. Of course, that would mean he had to actually go through with his plan to retire instead of putting it off for yet another year. Don't get me wrong, I love workin' with my dad at the garage, and it'll be hard to lose him, but at this rate, I can't wait for him to retire. He's been workin' too hard for too long, and the man deserves a break," Tyler said.

I could sense the genuine passion and worry in his voice, and it only made him all the more endearing to me. A Southern man who truly gave a damn about his family? Sign me up. Behind me, the oven beeped to let me know it was properly preheated. I arranged the peeled and diced potatoes on a baking sheet, drizzled them with olive oil, sprinkled seasonings over them, and put them in the oven, setting a timer for fifteen minutes.

"I can definitely understand the urge to work yourself too hard," I admitted. "Over the past few years, I've been working full-time at the gym as a personal trainer, but I've also been taking online courses to become a licensed physical therapist."

"Wow. That sounds intensive," Tyler said, leaning forward with interest.

I nodded as I cleaned the mushroom caps over the sink.

"Yeah. It's a lot. But in a small town like Winchester, there aren't any specialized physical therapy options. The only place in the area with the proper equipment just so happens to be the gym where I work. So I would be able to take on patients there, under the supervision of their primary care doctor, of course," I explained.

"Damn. That's some serious dedication. And with how important sports are to the community here, I bet you'd have a long list of clients in need of help," he said.

"Exactly. I mean, I'm sure you remember what it was like to be on that football team. If you got badly injured, there weren't a whole lot of options without having to drive to the city for hospital visits. I consider it my duty to deliver quality therapeutic care to the people of Winchester. They deserve a place locally where they can heal and improve themselves," I rambled passionately.

Tyler grinned, his eyes glimmering with warmth and appreciation.

"I couldn't agree more," he said softly. "Especially since my dad has his back issues, I know secondhand how life-changing injuries like that can be."

"Thank you," I said as I minced the garlic. "Anyway, the past few years I've been fortunate to take online courses. That way I could do the studying, testing, and group discussion from the comfort of my couch. My professors have always been very understanding about my work schedule and everything, which is nice. They work with me to get my schedule sorted out, and I've even had a few Skype sessions with my instructors to stay on top of things and ask for extra help on assignments. It's been a lot of fun, to be honest. I love school and learning new things, especially since this is where my passion lies."

"I'll bet. If I could take classes on how to be a better mechanic, I think I'd jump at the chance. I miss the days when I used to have time for reading and learning." Tyler sighed. "Nowadays, I spend most of my time hunched over a car or underneath one. Don't get me wrong, I love my job and I'm pretty good at it if I do say so myself, but I would love to improve my skills."

"It's been really rewarding," I said humbly. "But this final semester requires me to be on the community college campus near town three times a week for night classes. In person. So that's been a whole new strain on my weekly schedule. And now that my car is having trouble, I'm a little nervous about how I'm going to make it there for classes. If I can't attend those courses in person, I'll fall behind, and I don't want to risk losing all those years of hard work just because I don't have reliable transportation at the moment. But I'm determined. I'll figure something out. Hell, I'll take a taxi to and from work and class every time if I need to. This work fuels and motivates me to be better, and I'll always find a way to make it work. I can't give up now, not after I've poured so much effort and soul into my career."

I finished prepping the vegetables, flipped the potatoes around for more even cooking, put the baking sheet back in the oven, and began sizzling some turkey bacon in a skillet.

"Good gracious, that smells heavenly," Tyler groaned, taking a deep whiff.

"Nothin' better," I agreed. "And that reminds me, I can definitely help you come up with a plan for weekly exercise and meal prep, as well as a sleep routine that will help you get back on track for the big game. I can lay out a daily meal plan with rough caloric intake and balanced nutritional content, as well as a slowly increasing regimen of cardio, weight-lifting, and other mixed exercises like swimming and hiking. It'll be great."

"Hmm," he murmured, scratching at his chin thoughtfully. "See, that all sounds so fantastic, Mason. But the problem is I don't live alone. I live with my parents. My parents are early to bed and early to rise, but not to the extent that I would probably have to be to keep up with your plan. Besides, I don't exactly have free rein over the kitchen. Mom is a diehard home chef, and I think if I tried to usurp her culinary throne, she might lose her mind."

I chuckled. "Yeah, if there's one thing I know for sure, it's to never come between a Southern lady and her kitchen. Not if you want to escape with all your limbs intact."

I added the garlic and onion to the skillet, then the mushrooms, tomatoes, and collard greens, sprinkling them with more seasonings as it all cooked together. I took out a carton of eggs and took the sheet out of the oven, scooping the perfectly crisp diced sweet potatoes into the skillet with the rest of the veggies and the turkey bacon. By now, we had both polished off a couple of beers on an empty stomach, so we were feeling a little loosened up. As I cracked four eggs into the skillet, Tyler let out a heavy sigh.

"You know, Mason," he began, his cheeks burning a ruddy pink, "your plan sounds really amazing and well thought out, but the problem is... I just can't afford a personal trainer at this point in my life. I couldn't pay you what you'd deserve."

"Well, I find myself in a similar predicament," I confessed. "Because I desperately need my truck to get fixed, and I also need a way to get to and from my job and my night classes, but I don't think I can afford all that, either."

I put a lid over the skillet to help cook the eggs more evenly, and for a few moments, the kitchen was eerily silent. I could almost hear the cogs turning in my mind and in Tyler's mind as well. Then, at almost exactly the same time, we broke the silence.

"What if we make a trade?" Tyler said.

Simultaneously, I said, "I think we could work this out."

We both looked at each other a little bashfully, both blushing like schoolboys.

"Are we on the same page here?" I asked. "Dinner is ready, by the way."

Tyler came around the counter, and we each piled up our plates with the delicious sweet potato breakfast-for-dinner hash, then sat down at the small dining table in the adjacent room. We chatted and drank more beer as we ate, discussing our new plan in more detail.

"So you need a trainer, and I need a mechanic with a reliable car," I remarked. "Sounds like we have the makings of a quid pro quo on our hands here."

Tyler laughed, his eyes lit up with happiness and a tinge of tipsiness, too.

"Exactly. So I'll work on fixing your truck as well as drive you to and from work and classes," he offered.

"And I'll be your live-in coach, helping you stick to a diet, sleep, and exercise regimen that will get you totally pumped up and in perfect shape to take on the other team in the big game," I added.

"So we can both show off our vintage autos and our beefed-up bodies," he joked.

"Yep! Damn. Sounds like a plan to me," I said.

We finished up dinner and went to the kitchen to wash dishes and clean up the mess, both of us still chatting and dare I say, even flirting, as we worked side by side in the kitchen. With the beer freely flowing and our close proximity, I was beginning to feel truly hot around the collar. I couldn't deny it—I found Tyler deliciously, undeniably attractive. My body was drawn to his in a way I didn't come across often. Maybe it was the thrill of a well-laid plan. Maybe it was the lowered inhibitions. Maybe it was just pure, unadulterated physical attraction. But whatever it was, I found myself inching closer and closer to Tyler until finally we were standing shoulder to shoulder by the sink. I was washing; he was drying.

I accidentally – on purpose – bumped his shoulder with mine. He instinctively turned to glance at me, his eyes lidded and reflecting the same lust that coursed through my veins. My heart pounded like crazy, and time itself seemed to slow down as we moved closer together... and my lips pressed against his.

TYLER

It was as if the tension that had been hanging between us all evening had snapped, and the whole room melted into a fuzzy mess of warm sweetness that filled up my heart so full that I felt it ache. Was this even really happening? Were Mason Glass's full, pink lips kissing mine in the middle of his kitchen, with the muffled dialogue of Bannister Heights coming from the living room?

I wanted to bring my hand over to my arm and pinch myself to make sure this wasn't some bizarrely elaborate trick my mind was playing on me, but I couldn't. Mason's arm was already covering mine, wrapping around my body to reach my ass and grope me. I let him, too. I let him do whatever he wanted with me as he pushed me back against the counter, and I yielded to him when he pushed my arms aside to feel me up better.

We barely had time to breathe through our kiss. My mind was a melting storm of red-hot feelings that Mason had managed to stir up with a single gesture. I had spent the entire evening telling myself that I had been imagining things. This was the kind of thing I would fantasize about in the safety of my own head when I spent long hours bent over a car's engine, but I'd never expected it to be a reality. It wasn't that I thought it couldn't happen. Just because I liked the idea of a man in my life didn't mean I wasn't able to go out and get one if I set my mind to it. But Mason? *The* Mason? The guy everyone in our graduating class wanted to either be or be with?

After what felt like an eternity, Mason broke the kiss softly, then looked at me with lidded eyes and those hungry lips hanging open just enough to show the pearly teeth behind them. His eyes looked at me with more than just desire. I was in his territory, his home, under his roof, and I had just filled myself up with his food. He was my host, and the idea that I was something in his house that he could enjoy himself with at his leisure thrilled me. I couldn't deny it. Any pretenses of trying to keep my composure were quickly going out the window, no matter how fast I was trying to get a hold on myself again.

Mason and I had just shared a kiss, and he had made the first move. I had given the guy a ride, and he had turned my world upside down.

"What did you think of that?" he asked in a tone dripping with desire for more.

His question took me by surprise. What did I think? For a moment, I heard the question as if he was asking for a review, which didn't help get my thoughts in order. What should I have said? *Excellent, highly recommended, 10/10?* No, Mason's question was more carefully worded than I gave it credit for, and that told me Mason was far more than I bargained for.

"I need to know a little more before I make that call," I heard myself say, but I could barely believe those words were coming out of my mouth.

Mason couldn't either. The grin that spread across his face felt like that of a hungry lion sizing me up and realizing that I wasn't just prey. I might just be someone to contend with. An equal, even. His hand was still on my ass, and he reminded me of that by caressing it and giving it a slow, firm squeeze. It was the kind of feel that showed me exactly how much attention he was paying to my body and how much he admired it. I felt almost ashamed of myself for reading that much into a single copped feel, but I couldn't help it around Mason. The man had a way with the human body that went beyond what I was experienced with.

"Then why don't I show you a little more?" he offered, and he took my hand in his.

I followed him out of the kitchen in a daze, and he led me back to the couch in the living room. The fact that Mason kept such a clean and well-maintained house added to how much this whole experienced dazed me. It felt sinful and exciting, doing something so wild and out of character for me in a lovely home like this. I didn't know where I'd expected something like this to happen, of course. Maybe I had dreamed up something spontaneous happening in some shady bar or a messy studio apartment, somewhere that matched how this all felt.

Mason's hands held my hips, and he spun me around once we were at the side of the couch. He set me down on the arm of the couch, and I gripped the back with one hand while the other held Mason's back as he pressed a deeper kiss to my lips. This time, with his muscular body looming over me, I felt a thrilling shiver run up my back as he leaned into me. His tongue brushed against my lips, and I invited him past them to meet mine. He liked that, and he rewarded me by tightening his grasp on my waist. I felt his thick, strong fingers massage the sore muscles down there, and I squirmed to feel more of him and give him more of me.

I was a big guy, so I had never thought of myself as offering my body up for someone else to enjoy. I liked how I looked, but it had just never crossed my mind that a guy like Mason would not only want to do this to me but that he also would go out of his way, taking such a thrilling chance and hoping that I felt the same way that he apparently did.

If the cardio Mason was going to plan out with me didn't burn some energy, then the way he was getting my heart pounding on his own would do just fine.

Mason's hand wandered up to the small of my back, and he positioned his legs so that he could pull me in closer to him. I smelled his natural scent, that raw and untamed hint of a masculine smell that made my cock pulse between my legs. A moment later, I realized why Mason had moved his legs like he did. My cock's simple twitch was right up against his thigh, and my cheeks burned at the realization that he knew just how turned on I was. As if he could read my mind, he turned his hips so that I could feel *his* hardness, and I thought my heart was going to pound its way out of my chest.

His large hand wandered its way up my back and formed a claw that he dragged down slowly, raking his nails across my skin through the thin fabric of my shirt. I felt goose bumps on my arms as he pushed us closer together, so close that every little motion of my hips couldn't help but rub our bodies together, and each time that happened, I felt almost dizzy with desire for him.

His lips left my mouth with a hungry reluctance. His five-o'clock shadow tickled my face as he kissed my cheek, but that cute and almost innocent touch gave way as soon as he found my jawline, then my neck. I felt him bite me, gently at first, then more aggressively. My mouth fell open, and I gripped the couch so hard I was worried I was going to tear the upholstery.

Mason put a knee up on the couch and pushed me back so that my shoulders were pressed against the back of the couch. The awkward angle confused me for a moment, but then I realized that he had a firm, secure hold on me. Not only was I not going anywhere, but Mason now had my entire front exposed to him, and I didn't have anywhere to squirm away. And that was perfect. Everything about my words and my body language had told him to keep going, and I had no intentions of stopping that.

He started grinding against me, and our shafts brushed against each other through the denim of our pants. I felt myself go weak at that, and I gave a desperate groan as his teeth worried the skin at the nape of my neck. He began moving his hips back and forth in a steady rhythm, and the thick bulge of his cock stroked mine with such a relentless, agonizingly slow pace that somehow managed to tease my body to the point that my chest felt tight.

I was going to lose control if I wasn't careful here, but I was well past the point of caution. I slowly brought my hands up to his body, and starting at his hips, I began my own exploration. My hands wandered up under his shirt, and he made no move to stop me. In fact, he seemed to find it amusing. I felt his lips curl into that mischievous smile again as he turned to give me a better angle to touch him. My rough hands wandered up his warm skin, and immediately, I felt what I had been filling my steamiest fantasies with for ages.

His body was hard and soft at the same time, so firm with just the right amount of supple give. His muscles were toned beyond perfection, as far as I was concerned. Maybe there was someone with a scientifically more perfect body out there, but to me, there was only Mason the high school heartthrob. The curves of his abs felt so tight and intricate that I could have run my hands over them all night. I went up his front and over his pecs, and I could feel them moving in perfect harmony with his arms.

When I reached the zone where his pectoral muscles met his shoulders, I started to retreat, but Mason sensed my intentions beyond what my brief moments of hesitation kept me from acting on. He pulled back and lifted his shirt up over his head and tossed it aside, then looked down at me to lick his lips while my heart melted. I had made an image in my mind of what his body looked like, and the reality blew that out of the water. He looked like a model for a gym, but without the sense that too much work has gone into perfecting the sculpture that was his looks. He carried that beauty naturally, and he could have been on the cover of a magazine as easily as I could see him sweating out on the football field with me.

"Had enough to make up your mind yet?" he teased, reaching down to run his hands through my hair. "Do you want this, linebacker?"

I swiped my tongue over my lips and tried to get my thoughts together over the relentless pounding of my heart. And just like last time, I felt overcome with a kind of boldness I didn't know I had always had. I reached forward and hooked my fingers in the waist of his pants, pulling him forward to make him bend down so deliciously close to me. We stared at each other for a moment while my thumb wandered down to stroke his cock, and I nodded slowly.

"What I want is to taste you," I said in a thick, husky tone.

Mason reached down and caressed my jaw in his hand, and he gave my lips a brief but powerful kiss. When it broke, he touched his forehead to mine.

"You're more of a handful than I'd expected, Tyler," he growled. "And unlike a lot of guys, I like surprises."

"You took the words out of my mouth." I chuckled softly.

"I'd like to see you try and take them back," he said, and he pushed me back onto the couch with a fierce kiss as our bodies fell into a lustful pile.

Mason straddled me, and I was pleased to find that my body was perfectly accommodating for him. His thighs hugged my sides as he let me work open his belt, and I threw it to the ground with his shirt. I unzipped his pants while he held on to the back of the couch with one hand and ran his other hand through my hair. I now had a goal in mind, and nothing could have held me back from getting it. Within seconds, I found the opening of his boxers, and his cock sprang free.

"Fuck," I said, unable to hold back at the sight of it.

His cock was longer and thicker than I could have hoped, but even more importantly than that, it looked *powerful* in a way I had trouble wrapping my mind around. Fortunately, my hand didn't have the same trouble, and I soon felt his rock-hard shaft twitching as I ran my hand up and down it. The warmth of my palm heated up his whole length from tip to base. I looked up at him and nodded, and in silent agreement, he carefully slid forward so that he could angle his cock down toward me.

I had no idea how I planned on handling this situation but playing things by ear was serving me perfectly. I opened my mouth and gave that beautiful head one more look before I took it into my mouth. My eyes shut for a moment as I tasted him, and as my tongue rolled over the tip of his cock, I felt his grip on my scalp tighten. He groaned with me as I brushed my tongue under his bulging crown, and I opened my mouth further to let more of him in.

As I did, I opened my eyes and let my gaze wander down that shaft to his hips. The simple raw power that those taut muscles showed off was more than I knew how to process. My mind was reeling with electric thoughts that flew through my mind at a mile a minute. He didn't have to rock his hips anymore, but he somehow moved just gently enough that it helped my tongue do the work it was best at all along that thick shaft. I moaned into it as I pushed the tip of my tongue along the underside of his cock, but he got greedy soon and pushed more of him into me.

That made my heart do a flip, and I met his challenge. I tasted the base of his shaft at the same time that I felt his cock throb against the back of my throat. I had perfect control over my mouth and its reflexes, and I had no problem massaging his cock back and forth, building his tension ever more with each new thrust.

"Goddamn, Tyler, you're going to make me come," Mason growled. "I've been thinking about this from the second you let me into your car."

Fire was welling up within me. It was that feeling of having been pushed to the brink of excitement so many times in such a short amount of time that it felt like it all had to find escape, and Mason was that escape for me. I got faster, lavishing his cock with attention while my hand pumped his shaft at the base. I focused on his tip, wanting to drink every drop he was holding back from me. I wanted to give him something to remember, something that both of our bodies could thank us for later.

A smile came to my face unbidden when I felt his balls tightening, and he gripped my short hair with a sharp hiss, and I felt a splash of precome wet my tongue just seconds before a warm, delicious burst of this powerful man exploded into my mouth.

I held on, letting almost all of his cock out of my mouth so I could hold it with my hand and massage every last drop from him. His balls worked hard to empty themselves into me, and I drank from him deeply, groaning with every shot.

When his orgasm came to an end, my mind hadn't stopped racing any more than my heart. He slid out of my mouth slowly, and I watched his satisfied cock bob gently, glistening before me as Mason gazed down at me with a contented smile.

43

"I'm glad we're on the same page," he purred. "I was starting to worry I was making things up in my head."

"Me too," I murmured with a faint laugh.

"Now, why don't we see about you?" he offered, sliding his cock back into his pants and looking meaningfully down at my bulge.

For some reason, that alarmed me. I wanted it, desperately, but the reality of the situation was rapidly setting in. I had just done something wild and impulsive with Mason, and as sweet as it felt, my mind was scrambled eggs, and I didn't know what to do about it. I needed an out, and quickly!

"I would, but it's getting late," I said, pushing myself up slowly and smiling.

Mason looked somewhat surprised, but he nodded, getting off me and watching me as I sat up and stood to my feet.

"Is everything okay?" he asked, tilting his head to the side.

"No- I mean, *yes*." I chuckled, flustered, and to drive the point home, I stepped forward and kissed him for longer than I should have let myself.

Mason ran a hand up and down my back, and when I broke the kiss, he smiled.

"Just making sure," he said. "See you tomorrow, then?"

"Yeah," I said absently, scratching the back of my neck with a stupid, boyish grin and a blushing face. "Bright and early."

"See you then," Mason said with a chuckle as I made my way out the door, and before I knew it, I was hurrying out to my car.

Oh god, I hadn't even thanked him for dinner before leaving! No matter, I was too far out now. What was I doing? Trying to be a tease? Panicking? Taking a second to get my bearings? All of the above? I had no idea, but soon, I was in my car and heading home with my mind moving no slower than before.

What the hell had just happened? Did I really just give Mason Glass the best oral I'd ever had? A smile crossed my lips as I drove through the dark night, watching fog roll past me as my car picked up speed. I was stone-cold sober, but my mind was spinning nonetheless. When a deer bounded across the road ahead of me, as they often did on nights like this around Winchester, I nearly slammed on the brakes in overreaction.

Running out in a hurry was probably unnecessary, and I hoped I hadn't just made things awkward with Mason, but what I had just experienced was unlike anything I had been prepared for. I was a guy who liked a somewhat quiet life. I liked cars, and I liked hot men. Getting pushed down onto a couch by one and tasting his pearly reward for it was the last thing I had been expecting tonight.

But halfway home, a huge, sloppy grin spread across my face, and I realized I had to laugh at the absurdity of tonight. Things had exploded into a frenzy of passion in an instant, and it had all ended just as suddenly. Of course, anxiety was the next thing to hit me. When I pulled my car to a stop in my parents' driveway, I had to take a moment to breathe and collect myself before getting out.

I lived with my parents not because I couldn't afford my own place but because they were getting on in age, and I liked to be able to keep an eye on them and take care of things around the house or yard when I had time. Even though we practically had two sides of the entire house to ourselves, it still made situations like this a little awkward.

Taking up Mason on his offer to be roomies for a while sounds a lot more tempting now, doesn't it?

I blushed at that dirty thought as I slipped my shoes off and made my way through the house quietly. Once I was in my room, I felt bittersweet because while I was finally alone with my thoughts… that was just the problem.

I was alone with my thoughts, and I had to make a decision about whether I was going to meet Mason for jogging tomorrow when I'd just tasted him on my lips.

MASON

IT WAS THE KIND OF EARLY, BRISK SPRING MORNING IN WHICH THE world was blanketed in a heavy fog, clouding around the trees and houses like a massive curtain to shield the tiny town of Winchester from the rest of the world. It had been so cold when I woke up this morning that it was my shivering that shook me out of a dream. It had been a damn good dream, too. I was on the side of this lush green mountain, the air clear and bright, and we could see for miles around. In my dream, I had been on this journey not alone but with someone who had wiggled his way into my mind and made a home there: Tyler. I just couldn't get him off my mind, no matter how many times I tossed and turned in the night, no matter how fervently I tried to remind myself that this was a business arrangement, a working partnership, and not some serendipitous romantic meet-cute. I had not gotten as much sleep last night as I usually did. I had been in the world of physical training, nutrition, and healthy living for long enough to know the importance of a good night's sleep, but no amount of book smarts on the topic could help me nod off when there was something weighing so heavily on my mind.

I couldn't believe that I'd crossed such an important line. I had edged just over into the territory of no return, and now I was worried that my split-second decision would spell the end for my arrangement with Tyler before it even got a chance to start.

Way to self-sabotage, I thought to myself wryly.

Maybe this was just what I'd get for daring to muddle work with pleasure. I crawled out of bed, still shivering, and walked over to turn up the heat. I slid my feet into some fuzzy slippers and padded across the room to my closet. I yawned and stretched as I pulled out a pair of jogging pants, some thick wooly socks, my athletic running shoes, and an oversized gray fleece sweatshirt.

I hastily got dressed, my heart feeling so low it might as well have been dwelling inside my abdomen. I was nervous. Very nervous. Because this morning, Tyler was supposed to come over before work so we could fit in our very first jog together. It was meant to be a fun, easy wake-up session to break him into the routine gently and gradually. I had really, really been looking forward to getting to show him around my neighborhood, point out the houses I liked, and just chat about everything and nothing at the same time. The short of it was that I just wanted to spend some time with him. More time. Always more time. I couldn't get enough of the guy, but after our little stunt last night, I was afraid I might have spooked him away forever. It was difficult for me to determine who was at fault. After all, I had made the first move, but then it had been Tyler, who put the moves on me next, and he had taken it quite a bit further than I'd intended to. I could still so vividly recall the sensation of his mouth, warm and wet, stretching to accommodate the girth of my cock. A shiver ran down my spine at the image of gorgeous, handsome, shy Tyler bobbing up and down on my shaft, the little sighs and moans he made that vibrated up through my core.

Yikes. I needed to get a grip on myself if there was going to be any hope of getting through this business partnership without the two of us falling back into bed together.

I pulled a hat on to keep my head warm and, giving the clock on the wall one last forlorn look, I stepped outside and jogged to the end of my driveway to wait. I stood there, rubbing my upper arms to warm up as I squinted down the road to look for any sign of Tyler's car, though the fog was so dense I could hardly see ten feet in front of me.

Man, I hoped he would show. Not only because he was supposed to be my ride to work in a bit, but because I desperately wanted a chance to talk to him about what had happened last night. I wanted to set the record straight and reassure him that I could handle myself, that if he didn't want our relationship to develop in, well, *that* direction, then it didn't have to. I hoped he didn't regret what happened because I sure as hell did not. In fact, that kiss was the background film reel replaying again and again, projected onto the great wall of my memory. Maybe it wasn't the wisest decision. Maybe I could have waited a bit longer to make my move. But no matter how anxious I felt about it, one thing I did not feel was regret.

I crossed my fingers and murmured, "Come on, come on," softly under my breath.

A puff of warm breath crystallized in the cold fog for a moment and then dissipated. I shivered, wondering if I should have put on a thicker pair of running pants. Just as I was about to go back inside to retreat to the warmth of my house and change clothes, maybe prepare to call a cab to get me to work, I saw two watery white lights gleaming through the fog down the road. The lights were growing in size—no, getting closer. My heart leaped like a frog in my chest. Could it be?

I froze up, my heart pounding faster and faster as I recognized the car emerging from the mist as the classic Chevelle belonging to Tyler. I grinned and waved like a fool, too overjoyed and relieved to see him to play it casual. I had never been so excited to see a car in my life. I rocked back and forth on the balls of my feet, feeling like a weight was being lifted off my shoulders so I could finally breathe freely again. There was still a chance. Not all was lost.

He was wearing a big, beautiful, heart-warming smile as he pulled the gorgeous old car into my driveway. I listened fondly to the putter-putter of the engine, which I was sure had been lovingly restored and maintained over the years. If there was one thing I knew about car guys, it was how fiercely they adored and even doted on their vehicles. I had always appreciated that in a man, with the reasoning that any man who was willing to pour blood, sweat, and tears into a machine that would inevitably break down again in some degree had enough patience and passion to make a good partner romantically. I had yet to fully test out that theory, but it was on my mind as I jogged up to the driver's side door of the Chevelle. Tyler rolled the car to a stop, turned off the engine, and stepped out into the cold morning air, rubbing his hands together in their leathery gloves.

"Little nippy today, huh?" he greeted me.

I nodded, still beyond elated that Tyler was really here standing in front of me. And god, did he look absolutely delicious. He was a tank now just as he had been in high school, even if there was a little bit more pudge around the middle. He still looked like he could easily take down an opponent in a brawl if he wanted to, but from what I knew of Tyler's personality, that would never really happen anyway. He was the epitome of a gentle giant, every bit the linebacker he once was, but with a teddy-bear charm to him that made me ache with the desire to throw my arms around his body and hold him close.

"Yeah, it's a bit chilly. The weatherman lied again," I joked.

"To be fair, I don't think there's a meteorology program in the world that would take on Roger Ruff," he said with a laugh.

Roger "Ruff" Rudd was a bit of a hometown in-joke in a way. He had been the designated weatherman on the local news station for so long, at least as long as I had been alive. Even my parents remembered seeing him on television when they were young. He was known for his deep, gruff voice, his impossibly bushy white brows, his perpetually scowling expression, and for being serially incorrect about the weather predictions. The nickname was silly—it arose out of a local joke that he was actually a werewolf (evidenced by those bushy brows and his growly voice). From all accounts, he actually sounded like a pretty normal, friendly guy, and as far as I knew, he hardly cared about the nickname or his reputation as the worst meteorologist ever. But for born-and-raised Winchesterites, joking about the weather and therefore Roger Rudd by extension was kind of a given.

"Poor guy. I don't think he's been right even once in his life," I mused aloud.

49

"Yeah, but with how temperamental the weather is here in Winchester, I almost feel like it would be that way for anyone, not just him," Tyler quipped.

"You have a little more faith in the guy than I do, but it's sweet that you think so." I chuckled. "Anyway, let me first say that I am so, so glad you decided to come out here this morning, Tyler. I was really concerned that you might not show."

Tyler frowned and tilted his head to one side in confusion. "Really. Why not?"

"Well, because..." I paused, unsure of how to go about this. "Because of what went down between you and me last night."

An adorable flush spread across his ruddy cheeks. "Oh. Yeah. That," he murmured.

My stomach was twisting itself into tight knots of anxiety.

"So, what are you feeling regarding... that?" I pressed him.

He smiled softly. "I don't mind it. Well, no. It's more than that, actually. I don't really know how to feel about it other than just how I wish it would happen again," he admitted in a quiet, almost bashful voice.

God, he was so damn cute.

"That's a massive relief to hear. Oh, you have no idea how worried I was about that," I blurted out, feeling all the tension whoosh out of my body. "Not that I regret what happened. Not at all. In fact, I would also love for it to happen again. I like you, Tyler. I like being around you. And I have no regrets about kissing you, about touching you, about you touching me... except that I was worried about how you felt."

He shrugged. "Hey, it happened. Can't take it back now. I won't deny that I'm attracted to you, Mason. That's probably pretty obvious by now. No point pretending otherwise. And besides, I'm a grown man. I can handle it. Although I suppose maybe we should cool it down if we're supposed to be working together on the Plan," he pointed out wisely.

As much as I wanted to argue and debate with him on that fact, I knew he was probably right. I was extremely attracted to him and pretty much every moment he spent close to me only made me want him more, but I had to remind myself why we were here in the first place. He was here to get back into shape for the big football match, and I was here to help him do that in exchange for saving my beloved truck and for driving me around town. I needed to keep my eye on the prize rather than on Tyler's perfectly round, taut ass. Although the latter was much, much more tempting on the eyes.

"By the way, I did want to apologize for dashing off so quickly last night without an explanation. That was irresponsible of me. I hope I didn't totally ruin your night," Tyler said.

I clapped a hand on his shoulder and smiled reassuringly.

"Of course, not. You're entitled to your reactions to stuff like that. And like you said, we're both grown-ass men. We can handle this— whatever it is," I proclaimed. "And for now, we've got a great distraction waiting for us: we are going on a jog."

Tyler sighed, looking a little nervous. "Yep. A jog," he agreed, sounding utterly blue.

I chuckled and nudged his arm with my elbow.

"Come on. I promise I'll go easy on you to begin with. We'll do some stretches and walking to warm up before we go any faster. Sound good?" I said.

He looked slightly assured. "Okay. Yeah. Sounds great."

"All right," I said, stretching my arms up over my head. "Let's get started."

I took him through some basic stretches and yoga poses just to open up his core and tap into those lesser-utilized muscles. I needed his body fully woken and warmed up before we started jogging. Even a guy like Tyler, who as a former linebacker knew how to exercise, still benefited from easing into the more hardcore cardio. I was deter- mined to do everything exactly right. I was not going to push him too hard and risk an injury that would become a setback. I was going to ease him into it, pushing him along just hard enough to make steady progress. Before long, we were buzzed up on a rush of endorphins, and it was time to go. We fell in step together as we jogged around the neighborhood. He was breathing heavily, more concentrated on keeping up than holding a conversation. I pointed out houses I liked the look of and made small talk that didn't require long-winded answers from him. The point was to distract him from the discomfort of his burning legs and lungs, his pounding heart, the cold air whipping around his bare face. Once we had gone around the block three times, I called an end to our morning session, and we headed back into my house so we could shower off and get ready for work.

There were two bathrooms in my house, but only one shower, so we found ourselves presented with yet another conundrum. We were in a time crunch, both of us needing to shower off before starting the workday.

"You should go first," Tyler said. "It's your house."

"No, you should go first because you're a guest here," I said, our combined Southern manners clashing against each other in the fight for chivalry.

I glanced at the clock. "I suppose... no. That would be dumb," I said.

"What?" Tyler prompted, taking a step closer to me in the small bathroom. He was quickly pulling off his clothes, and I swallowed hard, trying to restrain my desire.

"I was going to suggest maybe we could share. But that's way too inappropriate," I said.

"Is it? I mean... it's better for the environment to shower together," Tyler piped up.

I laughed, starting to loosen up a little. If Tyler was fine with it, then why shouldn't I be fine with it, too? I slowly began to strip off my sweaty clothes as Tyler climbed into the steamy, warm shower. He groaned with appreciation as the hot water pelted his bare skin, and I could hardly wait to get in there with him. I parted the shower curtain and climbed inside, trying not to openly gape at Tyler's powerful, gorgeous body. He was a little soft in certain places, but that didn't bother me in the slightest. In fact, everything about him made me hungry for more than just that brief taste I had gotten last night. I stepped closer so that his body was nearly flush with mine, both of us sharing the stream of hot water. My heart was racing. His eyes pierced through to my very soul as we gazed at one another, frozen in place, both of us scared to make the first move. But then I felt my cock twitch against his slick thigh, and it was all over for me.

I reached up and cupped his face in my hands, leaning in to kiss him hungrily, almost desperately. He moaned against my lips and melted into my touch, letting my hands rove up and down his glorious body under the steamy water. I rutted against him, grunting as my cock slid up and down along his hip and thigh. I reached down and wrapped my hand around his stiffening cock, pumping it slowly and rhythmically as he groaned into our kiss. I slowly, carefully turned to press him against the glossy tiled shower wall, both of our bodies writhing in tandem. We were all riled up, the endorphins from our jog making us wild and needy.

"God, I want you so bad," I hissed between kisses.

"Me, too."

"I want to take you, Tyler. I want to make you feel so good," I growled.

"Do it. Take me. I want it, too," he shot back passionately.

That was all the encouragement I needed. I reached out of the shower and up to a built-in shelf, taking down a little decorative box made by a local woodworker years ago. I opened it up and pulled out a condom, sliding it on over my cock. I turned back to the glorious sight of Tyler bending over, that round ass sticking out and waiting for me. He braced himself against the wall with his powerful arms, and he was glancing back at me over his shoulder expectantly. I had never seen anything so delicious in my life.

I licked my lips and grabbed some coconut oil from the shower caddy. I usually kept it around for hair and skincare, but... I knew it would be useful here, too. I scooped a little glob of the oil onto my fingers and immediately began massaging the tight band of muscles around Tyler's hole. He groaned and bucked against my touch, making me grin devilishly. I worked his perineum and opening until I had relaxed him enough to slip one, then two fingers inside. I gently slid my fingers in and out, hooking them at the tips to better stroke against that perfect place deep inside him. Tyler groaned and whimpered, his legs shaking as immense pleasure rolled over him. I couldn't wait any longer. My cock was stiff as a board, and my balls were tight and heavy. I needed a release, and so did he.

I lined up the head of my cock at his slick opening and slowly, gradually pushed inside, using my hands to hold his hips and steady him. I entered him in one smooth thrust that made him cry out and tremble with bliss. I felt his tight ass clenching around my cock, and it felt like heaven itself.

"Fuck, that feels good," Tyler gasped.

"It'll only get better," I growled back.

I reached around underneath him to stroke his dangling cock while I pummeled into him from behind. Tyler cried out and rocked back against me in desperation, clearly overwhelmed by these blindingly hot new sensations. I fucked him hard, my own needs overwhelming me and taking over until finally, at the same time, I felt his cock spurt hot spunk all over my fingers as I filled the condom inside him. We groaned each other's names, holding still through the delectable aftershocks of pleasure that held us in place. Finally, once we were calm enough, I slid back out of him and disposed of the condom before getting back under that hot water with Tyler. His chest was heaving, his beautiful eyes wide with amazement. We held each other close as I gingerly, lovingly washed his body and hair.

"Well," he said, "so much for putting our feelings aside."

"Are you okay? How do you feel?" I asked gently.

Tyler smiled sheepishly. "I feel... I feel great, to be perfectly honest. And uh, just in case there's any question left in your mind, let me assure you that I do in fact think I would like to move in here with you for the time being after all."

TYLER

My heart was still thumping against my chest when I turned the ignition of my car just a short while later. I knew my car so well that even having someone else's weight in the passenger's seat made a difference that I picked up on, and I had to admit, the feeling of my baby firing up with Mason sitting beside me was one I could get used to.

"I saw that," Mason said unexpectedly, snapping out of my half trance and making me look up at him in alarm.

"Saw what?"

"That look on your face," he said, smirking and nodding at the ignition. "I saw that spark in your eyes when you started her up. It's a good feeling, isn't it?"

"Never gets old," I said, grinning, and I carefully pulled out of Mason's driveway to start driving us toward the gym.

I might have had a job that kept me in one place in town for most of the day, but even so, mornings in Winchester were something special that I had come to appreciate. Mason hadn't been kidding about living on the far end of town, and as far as I was concerned, that was just more time to appreciate the beauty.

Springtime was in full swing, and that meant the whole countryside was positively bursting with life. Just about every yard we passed had its azaleas on display and in full bloom. A lot of homeowners used the vibrant flowering bushes to provide shade for their houses, and it drew a hell of a lot of pollinators, to boot. Violet and red flowers lined the yards, and the fragile voices of birds like blue jays and wrens dotted the air like melodies, both near and far. As we drove through a wooded stretch of road, we caught sight of a couple of hares darting out of view, and I had to admire the vibrant butterflies that were swirling around each other this time of year.

Pine was everywhere, of course, and it seemed like there was no time of year when pine straw wasn't on the ground, even when there was a bit of snow on top of it. But despite that, springtime had no problem breaching the layers of straw on the ground and showing off what the land down here was capable of.

"Days like this, I would have been tempted to skip school and hope nobody noticed me sneaking to practice after," Mason said, leaning back in his seat and smiling at the scenery. "Mind if I roll down the window?"

"Think it would be a crime not to." I chuckled. "I don't think I remember you playing hooky back then, though."

"Nah, I honestly don't think I would've if the chance had been there," he said. "It would have put too much at risk for no good reason. What about you? Did you ever skip just to go hit the lake and stretch out for a few hours?"

He rolled down the window, and the aromatic air from outside flooded the car. It mussed his hair just that slight amount that it could, given how short Mason's hair was, but the natural light gave his face this almost otherworldly glow that I had to fight not to stare at. I could get lost staring at Mason all day if he'd let me, but it wouldn't do me much good if I accidentally steered the car into Lake Wren while ogling him.

"Oh no," I said, shaking my head and chuckling at the thought. "I was pretty straight-laced back then. I was always afraid of what my parents would think if they caught me."

"Really? They're not mean or anything, are they?" Mason asked, and I couldn't help but notice what sounded like a hint of protectiveness in his voice that made me feel a little fuzzy, no matter how unnecessary it was.

"Oh no, much worse," I said ominously. "If I acted out, they'd just be all somber and tell me they were *disappointed* in me," I said in the same tone that I might have been telling a ghost story around a campfire.

"The worst!" Mason laughed. "The most terrifying words a kid can hear: 'We expected better of you.'"

"Ooh, I've got chills," I joked as we chuckled together. "But no, I'd always just felt like I wanted to go the extra mile to make them happy, so I stayed out of trouble. Not to imply you didn't, I mean. I was adopted, and they're a little older than most parents, so teenage-me was always kind of conscious of that in one way or another. They never made me feel like I needed to be, though. I got lucky in that department."

"That's really sweet of you," Mason said matter-of-factly, giving me a once-over that made me blush. "Not many teenagers put that much thought into how they act. Sounds like they had a good kid to work with. How are they these days? I know you mentioned your dad still working and all."

"They're all right, but Dad *does* need to retire." I chuckled. "I say I still live with them to make sure they're all right, but these days, I feel more like I'm there to just keep reminding them both that it's okay for them to stop working one of these days."

"That's an important skill," Mason said, grinning. "Not one we get taught very well. So, your mom works, too?"

"In her own way, yeah, which is how she always does things," I said. "She's a 'veteran' of Winchester's army of woodworkers. When she was younger, she used to do a lot of it. She was good at chairs. She really enjoyed making those. The rocking chairs on our front porch were made by her. These days though, she keeps things small. For the past five years or so, she's been doing little wooden knickknacks that she can sell and ship without much trouble online. You know, little sculptures of bears or bees, boxes for trinkets, even those funny-looking wands you've probably seen in honey jars."

"Awh, now that's just downright idyllic," Mason said.

"She's earned the right to be." I chuckled. "Dad spent a lot of his younger years overseas in the military. There's a box of old love letters between them in the attic, in a box Mom made herself."

"You're kidding," Mason said, looking touched. "That's... unbelievably adorable. Sounds like they've got a charming little slice of paradise."

"It does, doesn't it?" I agreed, smiling. "They have a good retirement waiting on them, if they'd just get around to it. But you know how working folks can be when they haven't known anything else. I was thinking about trying to set up Dad with a steady stream of junkers for him to work on while he transitions into relaxing. At least that would keep him from swinging by the shop 'just to check in' every day."

"Just make sure that workaholic urge doesn't rub off too much on you," Mason said with a pointed smile.

I opened my mouth to protest that there was no danger of that, but all I could do was grin because I knew it would have been a damn lie.

"Maybe a little workout is exactly what I need in my life, then," I said as we pulled up at the gym.

"By the way," Mason said, opening the door. "Are your parents going to be all right without you? I didn't want to sound like I was pressuring you or anything if you're needed at home."

"I'll talk to them about it today, but I don't expect it's gonna be a problem," I said, and he gave me a nod before leaning over and planting a kiss on my cheek.

"Then I'll see you this afternoon," he said, flashing me a grin and climbing out of the car.

I hadn't been exaggerating when I said my parents wouldn't have a problem with me moving out. In fact, it was probably somewhat of an understatement. We both gave each other plenty of space, but I often wondered if I was too protective of them. I couldn't remember the last time Mom or Dad had asked me for help around the house, and whenever I went looking for something to do, one of them had usually gotten to it already.

In fact, they were probably getting into the habit of not relying on me so that they'd have plenty to do when they finally did decide to retire.

The rest of the drive to my shop from the gym felt strangely quiet because I hadn't truly been alone with my thoughts in a while. I saw the usual traffic along the way. A school bus was making its rounds, and I could see the outlines of a crowd of kids being rowdy inside it. The mailwoman making her rounds along a strip of businesses was hustling from one door to the next. On the side of the road, I saw a sheriff who had been in the class two years behind me giving someone a ticket near a gas station.

Winchester life marched on with surprising precision, despite the occasional break from the daily routine. I wasn't sure how a sudden steamy morning in the arms of one unbelievable man fit into that picture of the quaint Southern hometown where I grew up, but honestly, it felt more right than I ever would have given it credit for.

I felt warm all over, both inside and out. Mason was a man whose sheer strength and force of presence were things I somehow felt like I knew I'd been missing my whole life, but I hadn't realized how satisfying it would feel. It had been spontaneous, it had made me feel energized and alive, and it had been a fierce reminder that you were never too old to have a crush on someone.

That all added up to a pretty great picture, in my book. But change was change, and any change was something I would have to ease into. And that started at home.

I pulled my car up next to my dad's and climbed out, relieved by the sights and sounds of the garage as I had always known it. One of my techs was at the garage going over something on a clipboard with a customer. Another was inside it, trying to get a small jeep lined up over the lift, while the owner anxiously talked with my dad, who I could see at the desk inside through the front window.

"All right, I appreciate that," the customer was saying when I stepped through the front door, and she had an appeased look on her face. "Thanks, Mr. Pearson. You said Tuesday?"

"If not then, we'll give you a call," he said with that charming, kind smile that had won over so many other clients in the past.

The customer walked out, and I nodded to her before crossing the shop to see Dad, who greeted me with his usual smile and a wave.

"Morning, son, I was wondering where you ran off to so early this morning," he said. "Coffee? New pot just finished brewing."

"Yessir, don't have to ask me twice." I chuckled, making my way over to the machine as I spoke. "Had to be up early to meet a friend."

"Goin' fishin'?" he asked. "Or is there something else y'all get up to that early in the morning these days?"

I blushed, mortified at the idea of giving the tongue-in-cheek answer.

"Jogging, believe it or not," I said with a smile that told Dad I was just as surprised to hear me saying that as he was.

"Jogging," he repeated, blinking a few times. "There's one I can't say I've done since I had to, but I'm guessing you didn't have to go running in fatigues, either!"

"No sir." I chuckled. "I, uh, I'm getting together with a few of the guys from the old football team. The fifteen-year reunion is coming up, so we thought we'd get a friendly game together. Thought I ought to get in shape if I want to keep up."

"Oh my lord, is it time for that already?" Dad said, running a hand over his face and laughing. "Well, darn, son, that's great. You made your mother and me proud as hell out there when you were in high school. You're still in pretty good shape though, aren't you?"

"I suppose so," I said modestly, rolling my shoulders back. "I'll be able to tell you tomorrow morning when my muscles decide whether they want to start aching."

"Oh, they will," he warned me, wagging a finger. "Icy Hot was your friend back then, and it will be again. And don't shy away from the Epsom salt baths. Your joints are just going to get stiffer from here on out."

"I'd like to think I'd hit my forties before I have to start worrying about that," I said as I grinned over a steaming cup of coffee.

"It'll sneak up on you." He chuckled. "Who all's going to be playing?"

"Well, I don't know too much yet, since Hunter seems to be putting most of it together," I said. "But for now, I'm just trying to get a little more flexible like I used to be with... do you remember Mason Glass?"

"Sure I do!" Dad said, leaning on the counter with a warm expression. "Quarterback, right?"

Winchester was a typical Southern small town. High school football meant a lot around here, and if you had been on the football team, that would have stuck with people for a long time.

"He's the one," I said, nodding. "I'm working on that vintage truck Chet checked in, and he's helping me train in exchange. He's a personal trainer, so it's kind of an 'I scratch your back' deal."

"Always seemed like he had a good head on his shoulders, Mason," Dad said fondly. "Glad you two are staying in touch. It's too easy to let your friends drift apart if you don't keep an eye on them."

"About that," I said sheepishly, scratching the back of my neck. "Part of this sort of... training regimen, if you wanna call it that, involves me living with him for a while."

That took Dad by surprise, and he raised his eyebrows.

"Well, damn, that's more serious than I thought," he remarked, stroking his chin and giving me a searching look. "Don't push yourself too hard."

"Oh, no, it's nothing like that," I said, shaking my hand. "Part of it is just getting me into a routine and sticking to it. I've gotten too used to unwinding with pizza and beer after work, and I'd never get my ass off the couch if I gave myself half a chance."

"Sounds like you know what you're doing, then," Dad said with a sage nod. "Stay focused and keep working hard, that's the trick. Simplest lesson and the hardest."

"Yessir." I chuckled, patting the desk.

"And you take care of that truck, young man," he said sternly, tacking on the last two words as a joke. "That right there is a thing of beauty."

"*Yessir,*" I said with a little more gusto, and he gave me a wink as I headed out the door to the back.

Dad was great, plain and simple. He was the kind of old-fashioned Southern gentleman who taught me the manners I had, and I knew how lucky I was to have him and Mom in my life. They'd adopted me because they were having trouble having kids of their own, and while I didn't feel comfortable spilling all my guts to Mason yet, especially not on a routine car ride after sex, I'd always held myself to a higher standard because of that. They had never made me feel like I needed to, of course. I couldn't have asked for more loving and accepting parents.

And breaking the news that I was going to be moving out, even for a short time, had gone about as nonchalantly as I'd expected. Dad was happy as long as I was happy, and I knew he and Mom were just fine in each other's hands.

I had nothing to worry about.

...well, nothing except getting distracted from the game plan by whatever I was starting up with Mason. Could I say I was starting anything with Mason? Was it too early to ask him about that? I ran a hand over my face as I knocked back about half my cup of coffee and got ready to get elbow deep in work. Staying focused today was going to be a challenge that I was not equipped for.

MASON

"EARTH TO MASON. HELLO. EARTH TO MASON," GIGGLED A HIGH-pitched voice somewhere off to my left. I shook my head and blinked rapidly, realizing that I had zoned out at work once again.

I turned around in my swivel chair at the front desk of the gym to see Kate and Liz, two of my coworkers, staring at me and wearing bemused expressions. I felt an uncharacteristic blush spread warmly across my cheeks as I noticed that they had been trying to catch my attention for a few moments while I was adrift in dreamland.

I couldn't help it. All I could think about was Tyler. It had been days since he first agreed wholeheartedly to move in and live at my place for the time being, and I was still reeling from that event. About a week had passed, but I was still just as giddy now as I had been at first. I couldn't get over it—having Tyler in my house, hearing his heavy, rhythmic footsteps down the hallway. Seeing his jacket hanging from an arm of the coat rack by the front entrance. Smelling his distinctive musky, delicious masculine scent around the house, on my couch cushions, lingering in the kitchen or the living room. I would never tire of sitting in the passenger seat of his gorgeous old Chevelle, watching those powerful, labor-calloused hands gripping the steering wheel as he controlled the machine with perfect finesse and patience.

I loved hearing him hum country songs under his breath when he thought I was out of earshot. Cooking dinner with him in the evenings was a smorgasbord of fun all itself. We would joke and chat, flirting back and forth as we worked in easy tandem in the kitchen. We would dance closer and closer to the edge of that hard boundary, then spin back away, teasing one another endlessly.

He knew just how to glance at me across the room and capture my attention, holding me captivated while he blushed, that genuine smile brightening the whole room. I would brush past him in the hallway or let my hand linger on his shoulder as I came to collect him for an evening jog. We rose in the early, pale hours before dawn and take to the well-beaten path around my neighborhood for a brisk, eye-opening run in the mornings. Sometimes, if we finished with time to spare, we would forego the usual protein bar-and-a-banana routine and take to the kitchen to whip up some egg white omelets, loading them up with sautéed veggies and zero-calorie hot sauce. We would stand in the kitchen to eat, leaning against opposite counters so we could chat about the day ahead or even just enjoy each other's company in the comfortable silence. I had worried a little at first that having Tyler around might feel like an invasion, like having such a big guy in my house with me would make it cramped or claustrophobic. But as it turned out, that couldn't be further from the truth. He fit into my universe, my schedule, my heart just as easily as though he was made for it. Like all along I had been floating through this world with a Tyler-shaped void in it, and I had had no idea until he came along and filled the niche so perfectly.

Honest to god, I was having the time of my life with him around, and every day we seemed to grow closer together, his life and mine knitting together into one cohesive, colorful blanket. I woke up smiling in the mornings these days, my heart already thumping in anticipation of another day with Tyler. In such a short time, he had managed to turn my life upside down and inside out, but I was loving it. Every moment, every day.

So it was no surprise that here, at work, my mind tended to wander a little bit.

"Sorry, Liz," I said with a hasty smile. "I zoned out there for a second."

"Uh-huh. We could tell. You were really out of it, eh?" Kate quipped playfully.

"What're you thinkin' about so hard?" Liz asked.

She was leaning with her elbow on Kate's shoulder. The pair of them had been dating for ages, and yet for the life of me, I couldn't remember when it had started. It was almost as though they had just seamlessly merged into one unit at some point without my noticing. Usually, it was kind of considered taboo to date someone you worked with, but here in Winchester, there were only so many places to work. It was a small town. The likelihood of ending up playing coworker to someone you were romantically interested in or vice versa was pretty damn high. Especially for gay women. So I was happy that Liz and Kate had found each other. And generally, they were pretty well self-motivated. They tended to compete with and build each other up rather than just distract one another from their responsibilities.

"Yeah, what's got you spacin'?" Kate added with a suggestive waggle of her brows.

I snorted. "Nothing. I'm just… just tired is all."

"Tired? You? Impossible. You're like the Energizer bunny," Liz said.

"I've got a lot on my mind right now, all right?" I replied, trying to avoid the topic I knew the pair of them desperately wanted to tap into.

They were good at their jobs and a vital part of the team here at the gym, but in the downtime between teaching yoga and Zumba classes respectively, Kate and Liz were indefatigable nosy nellies. They were clearly trying to get me to talk about Tyler.

"Like what?" they both chimed at the same time.

I laughed and rolled my eyes, standing up to walk away. "Nope. Not happening. We are not going to discuss my personal life on the clock like this," I said.

I strode over to the weightlifting area and picked up a couple of fifty-pound dumbbells. I started curling them down and up to my shoulder, facing away from the girls. But to my dismay, they weren't ready to give up that easily. It was a slow moment at the gym, with no classes running and no one-on-one clients scheduled for another half hour. In fact, it had been relatively slow all morning. Kate and Liz had already done a full sweep-clean of the gym once or twice, and we were all caught up on paperwork, so I couldn't even think of any busy work to pass off on them and keep them distracted elsewhere. Nope. I would have to just withstand their nosy probing and wait for a client to show up and rescue me from the two-on-one interrogation they clearly had planned for me.

Kate and Liz came trailing after me, arm in arm as they always tended to be. It was kind of funny to watch them together sometimes. Kate was extremely petite, a twenty-three-year-old who barely cleared five feet tall and probably weighed about as much as one of my dumbbells. Liz, on the other hand, was only four or five inches shorter than I was, which meant that she towered over her tiny girl-friend. Liz was thin and willowy, with the kind of rounded calves and biceps that indicated long hours of dance choreography. She was a couple years older than Kate, but still in her mid-twenties. She taught various dance classes at the gym, mostly Zumba. The two of them were into rock-climbing, as well as kayaking and biking. Over the years, they had both tried repeatedly to get me to go with them on one of these adventures, but even if I was okay with being a third wheel, I had a feeling our difference in age would manifest a little more prominently outside of work. I liked having them as work friends, but I usually liked to keep my work and private life separated.

Although my current situation with Tyler looked like the opposite.

Liz sat down on a gigantic orange bouncy ball used for ab work-outs while Kate leaned against the wall next to her. Both of them had their eyes fully fixated on me, waiting for me to elaborate. I sighed. I knew I wouldn't get any exercise done with those two teaming up on me, so I put down the dumbbells.

"Okay, just ask your questions," I relented, holding up a stern finger. "But I can't guarantee I will answer them all."

They both looked as though Christmas had come early.

"So, who's that guy who keeps dropping you off at work in the mornings and picking you up in the evenings?" Kate burst out.

"And what happened to the truck you usually drive? I love that truck," Liz mused.

"Did you get in an accident? Is that guy the one who saved you?" Kate rambled, her eyes wide as she stumbled down a rabbit hole of some romantic narrative she'd clearly concocted in her wild imagination.

"The truck is in the garage. No, I didn't get into an accident. The truck's just really old. It's a vintage car. That means it needs a lot of upkeep," I explained.

I felt a twinge of worry again. God, I hoped Tyler would be able to fix my truck. I had been doing my best not to obsess about it when I knew perfectly well there was little I could do about it myself, but it was hard not to worry. After all, that truck was my pride and joy.

"Then who is that guy?" Liz asked.

"He's a real cutie patootie, by the way," Kate gushed.

I chuckled. "He's just a... a friend. An old friend," I said cryptically.

"How old?" Liz pressed.

"He's my age," I said.

"No, silly, she means how long have you been friends?" Kate corrected with a giggle.

"We've known each other since high school," I admitted. "We played on the football team together back in high school."

The girls both gasped as though this was the juiciest piece of gossip imaginable.

"Football? Really?" Liz said in awe. "You played football for Winchester High?"

I raised an eyebrow amusedly. "Yes, I did. Why do you sound so surprised?" I asked.

"Well, because... you just don't strike us as the football type," said Kate gingerly.

"Because I'm gay? Come on, girls. You two of all people should be above that kind of assumption," I chided them gently.

They exchanged guilty smiles and shrugged. "Fair point, but you're not changing the subject that easily," quipped Liz.

"Yeah, we wanna know everything!" Kate exclaimed.

"Tell us all about your dreamy football boyfriend," Liz egged me on.

"What's it like seeing him again after all these years?" asked Kate.

"Did you two keep in touch since high school?" said Liz.

"Or did you drift apart and reconnect?"

"Did someone set you up on a date?"

"Oh my god! Was it a blind date?"

"Or did you match on that dating app? Oh, what's it called..."

"Timbr? Something like that. Oh, you have to tell us!"

"Wait—I have an important question. So, personality-wise, is he sweet like Abel Bannister or a bad boy like Adrian Bannister?" Liz asked.

"Ugh, that Jesse Blackwell," Kate groaned.

"You know there's a rumor he's moving into town soon, right?" Liz piped up.

Kate snorted. "Yeah. Sure. And rumors are always true here in Winchester."

"I can't tell if you're being ironic or not," I said.

"Ironic," she said at the same time Kate said, "Not."

"All right, it doesn't matter anyway. Tyler isn't like any character on that show or any other show for that matter. He's a real person. A good one." I laughed. "One question at a time, y'all. Is this an interrogation or a conversation, anyway?"

"Both," said the girls simultaneously.

I pinched the bridge of my nose and sighed, amused and exasperated. They really were insufferable. They were lucky I liked them so much.

"All right. I'm working with Tyler--"

"Tyler! His name is Tyler! We got a name!" Kate blurted out excitedly.

She and Liz gave each other an enthusiastic high five. I fixed them with a dubious stare, and they both pretended to zip their lips shut as I went on.

"So, Tyler and I are working on a fitness and wellness regimen to get him back in shape for an important football match coming up," I revealed. "We're going to attend our fifteen-year high school reunion, and the football players are getting together for a so-called friendly game."

"Fifteen years?" Kate repeated, wrinkling her nose slightly.

Liz nudged her. "Damn, Kate, don't call him *old*."

"Sorry. I didn't mean it like that," Kate amended hastily.

I laughed. "It's okay. Fifteen years is a long time. Too long, even."

"But you and Tyler are back together," said Liz.

"Oh my god. Did you guys date in high school?" Kate asked.

I shook my head. "No, no. It was never like that. Hell, I don't even know if Tyler was out in high school. Either way, it doesn't matter. We're not dating now either. We're just working together very closely," I explained.

"How closely?" Liz asked, narrowing her eyes and leaning in interestedly.

I scoffed. "You two are impossible, you know that?"

"Yep," they said in unison.

"Now answer the question," prompted Liz, who was rubbing her hands together like some kind of gossip-starved evil genius.

"Well, it's a very intensive regimen I've designed for Tyler, so in order to keep him on track, he is staying with me for the time being," I let slip.

All hell broke loose. Both girls jumped to their feet in excitement. I had no idea why they were so intrigued by my potential love life, but I decided to just attribute it to boredom. Man, I would've killed for a customer to save me from my interrogation.

Kate gasped, "He's living with you?"

"In your house?" Liz added, wide-eyed.

"Yes, yes. But it's not what you think, okay? It's just to make it easier for me to keep him on track. It's nothing dirty or whatever you guys have in mind," I lied.

"Sure. Whatever. You can stay in denial if you want, but I think we all know there's something more going on between you and your mystery footballer," Liz pried.

She gave me an exaggerated wink that made me laugh out loud.

"You're ridiculous. He's not a mystery, Liz. He's just a guy who needs a personal trainer, and I'm a guy who needs a ride. It's as simple as that. Quid quo pro," I said with a shrug.

"Quid quo pro? Hmm. Sounds a little risqué to me," Kate said.

I blushed, realizing the other meaning of the phrase. She was right, of course, but I didn't want *them* to know that. I was beginning to feel a little cornered, and I could sense some word vomit about to come up if we didn't cut this short soon.

"Come on, just give us some of the details," Liz prodded.

"It's really not a big deal, y'all. I promise. He's staying with me, and we do a lot of exercising together. We cook meals together, and I teach him about macros and nutrition and caloric intake. We chat and hang out. Watch movies. You know, just normal guy stuff," I said hastily. "Maybe sometimes we end up sharing the shower or something but only because it's more convenient and, you know, better for the planet and everything. It's all very casual and normal, and nothing is going on, okay?"

The girls both gaped at me, smiles of pure glee spreading slowly across their faces.

Oh dear. I had said way too much.

Thankfully, we were interrupted before either of the girls could press me for more extremely private information. A client came striding up to the front desk, and the girls rushed over to attend to his needs. I let out the whoosh of breath I had been holding and swiped at the sweat just starting to bead at my temples. Man, those ladies had really put me through the wringer. I picked up the dumbbells to put them in the rack just as Kate and Liz directed the client over to me. I grinned when I recognized the guy walking over.

"Mark! What's up, man?" I greeted him with a handshake.

He was smiling from ear to ear. "I'm doing fantastic, Mason. Just awesome. But I was hoping you might be free for a quick workout.

Things have gotten really hectic with work lately since coming back from Argentina, but I don't want to risk falling totally off the wagon, if you know what I mean." He chuckled.

"For sure. Although I bet you burned a lot of calories in Argentina, right? All that hiking and exploring the cities," I said conversationally.

He looked starry-eyed for a moment. "Yeah, it was amazing. The sky there is just... just bigger than it is here somehow. And of course getting to go there with Carter was just a dream come true. Being with my boyfriend in the country I always longed to visit was awesome. And he's a really good person to travel with. He's super organized and never gets overwhelmed, which is perfect because I tend to get really hung up on the details. But Carter is smooth sailing all the time. It's really reassuring," Mark gushed.

"Yeah, you need somebody to balance you out," I agreed.

"Exactly. My instinct is to over-plan every hour of a trip down to the smallest detail. But when I was feeling a little under the weather in Córdoba, Carter managed to get me to relax and just hang out in our hotel room ordering room service and binge-watching Bannister Heights for a couple days. I never do things like that. Normally I would have been obsessing over how many different museums we could hit in one afternoon. Somehow, he made it just as fun to drink yerba mate in our robes and watch Jesse Blackwell seduce a hundred women on that one soap opera," he said with a laugh. "Fun fact: they *really* love Bannister Heights in Argentina."

"Good to know," I said honestly.

It warmed my heart to hear that they were doing well. The two of them made a truly excellent pair, and I was always happy to see local people pairing off and building a life together here in Winchester. So many went off to the big city and never came home, so I appreciated those who stuck around to help make Winchester an even better place to call home.

I led Mark through our usual guided workout, helping him keep up the right pace. We did some jogging on the indoor track and then hit the pool to swim some laps. All the while, we chatted back and forth about his dating life with Carter, about his big trip to Argentina, and of course, about how Roger Rudd had gotten the weather wrong yet again. I never tired of these Winchester-centric inside jokes. I relished the reminder that we lived in such a small, tight-knit community who could all rub elbows and joke around together like one big family. There were so many things to love about my hometown, but I couldn't deny the fact that I loved Winchester even more when I had a guy like Tyler to enjoy it with me. I could hardly wait to get off work so I could see him again tonight.

TYLER

SOMETHING FELT DEEPLY PERSONAL ABOUT WORKING ON A TRUCK THAT A man like Mason loved so much. I was standing under the lift after finally having worked up the spirit to get my hands on it, but it had taken a lot of preparation beforehand. And by preparation, I meant standing there feeling like I was on holy ground, staring up at something that belonged to someone who was so fiercely protective of it that I almost hesitated touching it.

Most people didn't get that personal with their vehicles. I had always thought that was understandable. People had busy lives that kept their attention on a dozen other things at any given moment, and they were probably raised thinking a car was just something that mostly took care of itself. When you're taught to think a certain way, it's hard to break out of it unless you have a good reason for it.

That meant that, when any vehicle came through the garage, I had a pretty good idea of what it was going to look like under the hood, so to speak. The last person to have touched any given car's innards was probably me or one of my techs or a mechanic in another town.

A vintage truck with a lot of love in it was nothing like that.

It was like coming into a house a carpenter or an interior designer had poured hours of time and energy into and being asked to gut it for repairs.

I wasn't just working on a truck; I was being entrusted with someone's baby. And since that was the case, I didn't think there was anything wrong with taking a little extra time to wrap my head around everything. It wasn't like there were all that many ways things could look under there, but the little details made themselves known.

As I checked the brake lines, I saw what looked like traces of a very old handprint on the metal. It was caked over with a fine layer of dust from the road, but I had to grin to myself because it gave me such a clear picture. I could see Mason on a creeper—the little four-wheeled platform used to get under a car without a lift—reaching out and feeling his way around on a warm summer's day, casually running routine maintenance on his car to the sound of cicadas in the distance.

I pictured him wiping the sweat off his brow with one of those thick, muscular arms as he worked his way around his truck's underbelly, then pushing himself out and standing up, looking like a magazine cover model in a tight white T-shirt smudged here and there with grease, begging to get torn off as he stepped into a steaming shower...

I had to keep my head clear, and I was failing, which was not a surprise. Reminding myself that I'd be able to get my hands on Mason and hear firsthand what he got up to under this car, I gave my head a shake and got to work.

The day marched on, and I had a spring in my step all day long. I had set today aside to run a diagnostic, since our queue was hopelessly backed up, and I hadn't had half a chance yet. Maybe it was because I was able to work on something so personal to Mason, but this was the kind of day that made me remember why I became a professional mechanic.

I got to feel the snug grip of a wrench in my hand as I tightened odds and ends on Mason's truck or took pieces apart to inspect them for damage. The sounds of my coworkers were a constant presence in the background as the guys put the cars on the car lifts and carried on with everything from routine oil changes to coolant leaks to muffler replacements.

I loved the smell of rubber and grease, and the sound of a hydraulic lift and the buzz of an impact wrench were music to my ears. There was a simple beauty to putting your hands on well-loved metal and using power tools to whip it into working condition.

"You know," came a familiar voice from behind me, "I'm eyeballing everything you are under this here truck, and I've got to say, I don't think I've seen some of these parts up for sale anywhere in about ten years."

I turned around to grin at my dad, who was standing a few feet behind me with his arms crossed and his eyebrow raised. Above anyone else, Dad knew my penchant for biting off more than I could chew.

"Well, you're not wrong," I said, nodding at the truck I'd been working on for a few hours now. "But I know a forum on the internet where a lot of vintage car owners trade parts and keep an eye out for rare finds. I've had my eye there even before Mason came through with this job, so I think I might check in with some of my connections and see what I can turn up."

"Is this Mason fella all right with the bill that's going to rack up?" Dad asked, approaching me and standing by my side. "I figure he would, but you know how expensive it can be to go through private sellers like that."

"Oh, I'm sure he knows," I said as I stepped back from the truck, grabbed a towel, and cleaned my hands and forearms of the grease and grime. "He's put in his fair share of work with his own two hands... and his own wallet, I imagine."

"I just know how much you like to help people out." Dad chuckled. "Especially when they know their way around a car, even if it's only a hobby. Wouldn't want you taking too much out of yourself to impress, is what I'm gettin' at."

"Don't worry about that," I assured him. "I've done a little home-work on what this workout program of his might cost if we were handling this with cash, and trust me, this is a fair trade."

I wasn't exaggerating. Going to the gym for personal training was one thing, but I was getting the kind of treatment usually reserved for wealthy clients who could have staff in their house. I was sure Mason hadn't even thought of his work that way anymore than I would have reduced my work down to a series of price tags. Regardless, I felt very good about the fairness of our trade, plain and simple.

But Dad seemed to be angling for something else, and I couldn't quite place what that was. After giving me a judicious eye for a moment, he smiled and nodded away from the lift.

"Why don't we grab lunch? Looks like we've got a lull on our hands for a little bit. Might as well jump on it," he suggested.

"Yeah, my stomach's starting to growl," I admitted. "Don't want to let what I brought go to waste. If I leave it in the fridge too long, Chet might get to it. You know what he's like."

Dad chuckled with me as we went to get our hands and forearms washed up, then headed into what served as a break room and kitchenette in the back. The garage was nothing fancy by any stretch of the imagination, but it had everything we needed to run it efficiently, in a "rough and ready" kind of way, as Dad liked to call it.

There were two of the mechanics, Gavin and Tucker, getting up from the table as we entered, having just finished a quick lunch themselves.

"Did you hear Marshall's playing?" Gavin said as he tossed his trash away and gave us a quick wave as we entered. "Maybe we ought to back out if that beast's getting on the field."

"The bouncer? Shit, are you kidding? I can take him," Tucker boasted casually, and Dad exchanged a smirk with me.

"You can take him till I have to clean you off the end zone." Gavin laughed, punching Tucker in the shoulder. "I've seen him throw fellas twice your size out of The Chisel. Don't give me none of that 'size matters not' crap, either!"

The two guys were laughing good-naturedly as they slipped out of the room, and Dad chuckled as he went to the fridge. I took a seat at the end of the table with my mind now wandering to the game coming up, and I felt my heart thudding against my chest at the thought of getting back to training with Mason. I still felt the odd twinge of anxiety about getting back on the field, but the more time I spent getting in shape with Mason, the better I was feeling about it. It was a slow but steady process. Did that mean I'd feel good about going toe to toe with the likes of, say, Marshall the bouncer? Maybe, maybe not. It was still a long ways to the game.

"Y'all really got the town abuzz with your game," Dad remarked as he got our separate brown paper bags out. "Sounds like it'll really be something to watch. How're you feeling about this whole training you're doing for it?"

He set the bags down on the table and handed me mine. It was a simple but filling grilled chicken salad in a Tupperware container. I had put it in a brown paper bag so that the other guys wouldn't give me shit about eating something that wasn't doused in grease, but the look on Dad's face when I took it out of the container was priceless.

"Pretty good, all in all" I chuckled as I opened my meal.

"Must be, if that's what you've got for lunch," he said with a laugh. "I'm just teasin', though. This Mason guy isn't making you feel like you need to be eatin' like that though, is he?" he added with a suspicious edge.

It finally hit me what Dad was getting at, and my eyes widened for a minute before I smiled. He wanted to know how things had been going with Mason. I should have figured this talk was coming, but I had to wonder how much he suspected about us.

"No, not at all," I said, shaking my head. "That part is on me, really. Mason made clear from the beginning he –" I stopped myself short of explaining that Mason had been into my looks from the first second we'd met, but I couldn't say that to my dad. "That he didn't think there was anything wrong with me," I clarified. "He wants to help me reach my goals, so whatever goals I set for myself, that's what he helps me do. And it just so happens that some of my goals include not looking like I've been having as many beers in the evenings as I do." I chuckled, patting my stomach.

"Ain't nothing wrong with a little gut," Dad said, shaking his head and laughing as he took out his roast beef sandwich. "Hell, might even serve you well out there."

"I appreciate it. I really do," I said, "but don't you go worrying about me. I've got a handle on myself."

"That's good to hear," he said, trying not to let me hear the relief in his voice, worrier that he was. "So, how's the whole live-in situation working out? It's a little unusual for a guy to move in with his personal trainer, isn't it? Or is that a new thing?"

"I think just about anyone would call us unconventional," I admitted with a laugh. "I mean, us as in, our arrangement. Between professionals."

Dad peered at me with a raised eyebrow as he chewed a bite of sandwich, and I felt a mild blush on my cheeks as I realized I'd put my foot in my mouth.

"I just mention it because I can tell by the way you look at that truck of his, you must get along with the guy," he said.

Dad had a way of talking when he thought more than he was letting on. He would always avert his eyes, usually keeping them on something in his hands or nearby, and his tone made me feel like I was being taught a lesson of some kind. Dad had never been the best at subtlety.

"He's a good guy," I said, figuring now was as good a time as any to try and ease Dad into the waters of introducing him to Mason. "Driven. Guy who really knows what he likes and knows how to get it. He's an expert at knowing how the human body works best, so I feel like I'm in good hands. And I mean, he's the kind of guy who drives a truck like the one I've got on the lift back there, so that should tell you a lot about how he takes care of the things he likes."

"And does he take care of you?" he asked.

The question made my heart do a somersault, and I couldn't keep a smile off my face. Shit, apparently I inherited my father's skills at being subtle.

"Well, it takes a while to really get to know someone," I said, unsure if we were really talking about the workout routine anymore. "But it turns out we've got a lot in common. I wish we'd stayed in

78

touch more after high school. You'd love the guy. Is everything all right around the house?" I asked, hoping to move the topic away from coming so close to discussing my feelings for Mason.

I wasn't ashamed of what we had, of course, and I would have never thought for a moment that my father would be anything but happy for me. But I didn't want him to think I had just moved out of the house to immediately start rooming with someone I only just started dating. Mason and I weren't even dating! Were we? No, we definitely couldn't call it that. We had slept together, but all that meant was that we were into each other.

Sure, I had already come to know his morning routine. Sure, I noticed when he used a different conditioner one morning. Sure, the sound of his footsteps when he got up before me woke me up and got me excited to start the day. That meant I had one hell of a crush on the guy, but it didn't mean we were an item, did it?

"The house is fine. We just miss seeing you is all." He chuckled. "Well, your mom does, since I see you every day here. She wants to know about this mysterious Mason, too."

"Oh yeah?" I asked as I devoured my lunch.

Despite what it sounded like, the spicy mustard dressing Mason had whipped up made it taste pretty great.

"I think she's asking more about his looks than anything else," he said, holding back a bigger smile.

Yeah, Dad was definitely prying for information on my love life. I held back a smile that matched his, and I raised an eyebrow at him while I cursed my cheeks for showing some color. I opened and closed my mouth a few times, trying not to laugh, but when I realized Dad was doing the same thing, I couldn't hold it back. We laughed together, and I ran a hand over my now beet-red face.

"She can come see his looks at the game when we kick ass together," I said with a wink. "And that's the story you can bring home."

"Understood," he said, still smiling. "And hey, don't think I'll go spreading any rumors. I know how Winchester likes to gossip, but the buck stops with me. Just don't be afraid to ask for any advice from your old man. Not that you need it. You got a good head on your shoulders, and I'm sure you know what you're doing...in football," he added with a wink.

"Thanks, Dad," I replied, feeling warm and fuzzy inside.

I tried to find more to say, but Dad was contentedly eating, and I realized there didn't have to be anything more said. Dad had always been a quiet man when it came to personal matters like this, and I knew him well enough to recognize a blessing when I saw it. And that meant a hell of a lot.

Sometimes, there wasn't more *to* say than that.

MASON

Never before had I felt so lucky to work in a gym. Don't get me wrong. I always loved my job; I liked the can-do atmosphere, I loved being surrounded by people working hard to improve themselves and make progress in their fitness and lifestyles, and of course I adored my coworkers, even if they were a pain in the ass sometimes. But tonight, around the hour it came time for me to clock out for the day, I was most grateful for all the exercise equipment I could use to keep myself distracted. Instead of anxiously pacing back and forth behind the front desk like I had the urge to do while waiting for Tyler to show up, I could lift weights and jog on the treadmill. It was crazy— most days spent at the gym left me a little sore and exhausted by the end of the shift. After all, I tended to join my clients in their workouts, jogging alongside them or maybe doing some one-on-one kickboxing practice. Not all personal trainers did this, but I rather enjoyed the challenge of meeting my clients halfway. I believed that it instilled a strong feeling of camaraderie and teamwork between my client and me when we did the workout together, rather than me just standing on the sidelines shouting instructions at them. But today, not even a full shift of regular clients on fairly high-caliber workout regimens could burn off all the excess energy bouncing around inside my body.

Because every single time I had a spare moment to myself, all I could think about was Tyler. About seeing him again, hearing his soft drawling voice again, standing close and feeling the heat building up between us again. No matter how many laps I ran or how many dumbbells I curled, I was still buzzing with enthusiasm and anticipation by the end of the day. Even my coworkers had noticed the uptick in my energy level. Liz said I was acting "squirrely", and Kate described my demeanor as "a toddler who chugged a cup of espresso." Needless to say, I laughed out loud at their descriptions, but I couldn't deny it either. That was just the kind of effect Tyler had on me. All day long I kept obsessively checking the clock, waiting for the minutes to tick down to five o'clock, when I would clock out of my normal shift and jump into Tyler Time.

I couldn't wait for him to get here so we could get started on the aptly named Plan. I had enough energy for the both of us, but I hoped he wouldn't be too worn out after a day of being hunched over a car engine. In between clients I had sketched out a more finely detailed workout regimen down to the hour, along with some potential football plays to go over, and a descriptive meal plan outlined to the calorie. Admittedly, I was aware that calories weren't necessarily the most accurate or helpful way to look at food and health in the nitty-gritty sense, but it could help guide portion sizes and nutritional content as a whole, so it was a good starting point for someone taking on a new diet.

I was jogging on the treadmill when Liz came sauntering up to me with a smirk on her face, her arms crossed over her chest. She looked incredibly sassy, and I just knew she had some quip to toss my way.

"What is it?" I asked suspiciously.

"Nothin'. I'm just watching you run around like a hamster in a wheel." She giggled.

"Hey, we're surrounded by exercise machines. Why let it go to waste?" I said with a shrug. She grinned and shook her head at me.

"You've really got it bad for this guy already, don't you?" she pressed curiously.

I glanced around a little nervously, as though someone would overhear. She was right, of course, but I didn't exactly want my other clients to know I was having intense, distinctly unprofessional feelings for my main client.

"Maybe, maybe not. Either way, he'll be here any minute, and the last thing I need is for him to hear you say that," I said with a laugh. "I'm trying to keep things professional here, Liz."

"Sure, sure. Good luck with that," she said, giving me a playful wink as she walked off.

I sighed and shook my head, pumping up the treadmill to a faster pace to burn off my excess energy. A hamster in a wheel. I couldn't even argue with her on that. I knew how overly enthusiastic I must look to others. But I couldn't help it. Just thinking about Tyler made me happy. I looked at the clock on the wall and checked my phone again as I ran on the treadmill.

It was five after five, and I had a text message from Tyler.

My heart skipped a beat as I opened it. The message just read: Just clocked out. Will be there soon. Looking forward to seeing you!

I couldn't keep the goofy grin off my face. Man, this guy really had me wrapped around his finger. Already. Was I really such a hopeless romantic, or was this... something more? I did my best to shove that thought to the back of my mind for the time being. I would take it back out and inspect it later, but right now I had something else to focus on because Tyler had just come walking through the front entrance of the gym. My heart began to pound much faster than when I was on the treadmill. I turned off the machine and hopped off gleefully before straightening up and trying to casually meet him by the front desk.

Play it cool, Mason. Just relax, I reminded myself.

"Hey, man! Good to see you," I greeted him.

"Hey, Mace! How's it goin'?" he replied warmly, and I felt my heart flutter like a hummingbird at the nickname.

"It's great! I'm great. Just really pumped to get started on our Plan tonight," I said, totally incapable of disguising my excitement. "How was work?"

He shrugged good-naturedly. "Pretty good. I got a lot done, even managed to figure out a problem the other guys were stumped on," he admitted a little bashfully. He was always so incredibly modest, even to a fault.

"Wow. Not that I'm surprised. You're a genius with cars," I remarked.

Tyler blushed, and it was so damn cute I had to hold back the urge to cup that gorgeous face in my hands and plant a huge kiss on his lips. But I had to keep in mind that we were at my place of work, and I needed to keep things professional. Somehow.

"Well, thank you. I do my best," he said humbly. "So, what's on the agenda for this evening? I'm a little sore from work today but I'm ready to get goin'."

"Follow me," I said, accidentally catching Kate's eye at the desk. She was grinning broadly at the two of us, not even trying to hide her giddiness at watching Tyler and I interact like two shy teenagers. I wrenched my gaze away from her and led Tyler through the gym to the back, down a hallway and out to the indoor pool.

"I figured we'd start with swimming some laps tonight," I said brightly. "It's a great way to ease into a workout regimen, and it'll probably help alleviate some of those sore muscles. I want you good and relaxed before we move on to anything more strenuous. Sound good to you?"

"Of course," Tyler replied with a smile. "I'll go change real quick."

"Cool. I'll wait for you in the pool," I said, watching him rush off to the changing room.

Naturally, my mind immediately began to picture him in that changing room, stripping off his motor oil-stained clothing, getting naked, and revealing that glorious body. The little extra pudge did not bother me in the slightest. In fact, I just found it endearing.

I longed to wrap my arms around him and hold him close. But not now. Not yet. We had work to do. He came back out wearing swim trunks and a T-shirt, which kind of made my heart ache for him. I knew he was wearing that shirt because he wasn't completely confident about his body. But then again, that was where I came in. I was determined to not only get him back in fighting condition physically.

I wanted to give him more confidence and self-love. He was an amazing guy, and I considered it my highest duty to help him realize it.

"Is the pool heated, or is it freezing cold in there?" he asked as he walked along the side of the pool. I gestured for him to get in at the shallow end.

"It's heated, don't worry. I wouldn't make you swim in a frigid pool, I promise," I laughed. "I may be your fitness instructor, but I'm not here to torture you."

"I know," he said warmly, a glimmer of affection in his eyes. "I trust you."

He waded into the pool, the T-shirt slicking down to cling around his frame. I did my best not to ogle him as I began guiding him to swim laps. I was pleased to find that he was actually a pretty strong swimmer, which certainly made my job easier.

"You're a good swimmer," I remarked. "Have you done a lot of swimming in your day?"

Tyler nodded. "Yeah, when I was in elementary school we had a neighbor with a pool. I spent a lot of time at their house playing around in the pool while our parents grilled out and drank beer and listened to '80s music," he explained.

I chuckled. "Sounds like a really fond memory for you."

"Oh, yeah. Definitely. To this day, whenever I smell chlorine or smoking coals, I immediately flash back to those days swimming around in the pool with my neighbor. Her name was Constance. Can you believe that? Luckily for her, she went by Connie," he said.

"Constance. Wow. And she was our age?" I said, raising an eyebrow.

Tyler swam beside me in perfect form and said, "Yep. Actually, she was a couple years younger than me. I don't know why her parents gave her such an old-lady name."

"It's definitely unusual. But then again, in a town like Winchester... maybe not as surprising as it might be elsewhere," I mused.

"Anyway, that family moved off to Arkansas when I started middle school, and the family who moved into the house after them got rid of the pool. But by that point I was already a strong swimmer, so my parents and I would go swimming and kayaking in Lake Wren on camping trips. So I guess I've always been a pretty good swimmer. I definitely enjoy it," he said.

"That's good. Funnily enough, I actually didn't learn how to swim until I was eighteen years old," I confessed. "Don't worry—I'm a strong swimmer now. But I had a bit of a phobia when I was a kid."

"Really? A phobia of water?" Tyler said, surprised, as we came to the other end and turned to continue swimming. I smiled wistfully at the memory.

"Not so much water. I was actually just deeply, deeply terrified of sharks," I said with a laugh. "I saw the movie Jaws when I was way too young, and it kind of traumatized me. It was bad enough that I refused to take a bath by myself until I was, like, nine years old. I used to make my mom stay with me while I bathed just in case a shark might appear out of the faucet. And yes, I do know how insane that sounds."

Tyler chuckled, pausing for a moment to catch his breath. "No, it sounds adorable. You must have had a very active imagination," he commented.

I nodded. "Oh yeah. For sure. I was petrified of sharks in the bathtub, but I was convinced Lake Wren was infested with them, too. I used to just sit on the muddy banks while my cousins swam around without a care in the world. It's okay, though. I'm over it now," I said.

"I should hope so. It would be difficult to teach people how to swim laps if you were still afraid of a shark materializing out of thin air in the pool," he joked.

"Definitely. Fun fact: our old football coach used to try and urge me to join the swim team, too, but I always said no. I made the excuse that I didn't have time for it between football and homework, but the truth is, I just didn't want to be in the water," I said.

"I get that," Tyler said as we resumed swimming to the end of the pool. "Coach was always telling me to do track and field, too. He was convinced I would make a great pole-vaulter."

I snorted. "I didn't even know we had pole-vaulting."

"I don't think we did. That's why he wanted me to do it," Tyler said with a laugh.

"Ah, Coach. Good guy," I said.

"Yeah. We were lucky," Tyler agreed.

"I wish we had known each other better back in high school," I said suddenly.

He stopped swimming, treading water dangerously close to me. I could see beads of water tracking down the sides of his handsome face, his hair soaked and pushed back by the force of his breaststroke. He looked at me with those luminous, thoughtful eyes, and I felt like I might melt into a puddle of foam on the surface of the water.

"Me, too. I think we could've been really good friends," he said quietly. "I sure as hell could've used some more friends back in the day. Don't get me wrong, I was never bullied or anything like that, really. But I spent more time alone than was probably healthy for a kid that age. I was just so damn shy."

"You were always so quiet," I remembered. "Quiet and strong."

Tyler smiled. "And you were always so bright and optimistic. Some things never change. Thank god," he added warmly.

"Come on. I think you've done enough laps for the evening," I said. "Let's hit the showers and get that chlorine out of your hair before you turn green."

The two of us climbed out of the pool and walked back to the showers, dripping wet and shivering. I could plainly see the goose bumps prickling up along Tyler's arms and legs. Every fiber of my being urged me to wrap my arms around his frame and use my body heat to warm him up. Because as cool as it was getting out of the heated pool and back into the brisk gym air, I still felt pretty damn warm all over, and there was no question in my mind as to why. Just being around Tyler made me feel like I had a damn fever. My whole body heated up with lust and affection for this sweet, modest, strong man. Every time he looked my way or, god forbid, touched me gently, I felt my temperature rising. And of course it didn't help that in our clingy wet clothes, I could clearly see the outline of a thick bulge at the front of his swim trunks. I licked my lips as we walked into the locker room, my eyes following Tyler as he stepped into one of the shower stalls and pulled the white curtain closed. I got into my stall as well, though I couldn't quite tear my eyes away from him. To my delight, the curtains were not perfectly opaque. I could see the silhouette of Tyler's body through the white fabric, and my cock stiffened as I surreptitiously watched him lather up and wash his hair.

God, I was so turned on. My cock twitched with need between my thighs, and my hands itched to give myself some relief. All day long I had been thinking about Tyler. He was never far from my thoughts, circling around and keeping me in a state of semi-arousal pretty much from the moment I woke up in the morning until the second my head hit the pillow at night. Something about him just... hooked me. Before long, I found myself unable to resist anymore. I began to stroke my cock, every now and then peeking out from behind my shower curtain to catch a glimpse of Tyler's shape through his curtain.

"So about your truck," Tyler began casually.

I winced, knowing it was probably not cool for me to touch myself while we carried on a perfectly normal conversation, but I couldn't resist.

"Yeah? How's that going?" I prompted, still pumping my cock with one hand. I leaned back against the cool tile wall of the shower stall.

"It's going pretty well, I think. It'll take a lot of precise work, and I'll definitely need to order some specific parts that can be a little difficult to track down, but I'm confident I can get all the pieces together," he explained.

"Uh-huh. So you're saying she's fixable?" I asked, trying to keep the breathlessness out of my voice.

"Oh, for sure. It'll take some time, but I know I can get her back on the road," he said.

I bit my lip, holding in a gasp of pleasure as my hand slipped down over the sensitive, swollen head of my shaft. God, this was so dirty. I knew it was probably wrong, but I couldn't resist. I had been so riled up all day long just thinking about Tyler, and now that he was here, it was like my body just couldn't control itself.

"I'm really enjoying the workouts so far, by the way," he said sweetly.

"Oh. Good to hear," I managed to choke out as my pleasure mounted higher and higher.

I was getting close. I peeked out of the curtain to look at his silhouette again. I did a double take, thinking for a moment it looked as though Tyler was doing the same thing as me. But that couldn't be. Right?

"Yeah, I never really pictured myself as the kind of guy who goes to the gym regularly, but you make it seem a lot less intimidating," he remarked.

Warmth spread through my body as the shower stream pelted me with hot water, tracking down my frame as I stroked myself quietly. I bit the inside of my cheek to keep from moaning as I reached a crest, my come spurting sticky and slick over my fingers and down my legs. I let out a heavy sigh and let it all go down the drain, my chest heaving as I fought to hide my pleasure.

"You okay over there?" Tyler asked suddenly, concern in his tone.

Shit. I wasn't as slick as I thought I was, clearly.

"Oh, yeah! Yep. Yes. I'm totally fine," I said quickly.

We finished up in the showers and got dressed, my body thrumming with a glowing energy as we walked out to the parking lot together. I could smell the scent of Tyler's soap and shampoo, and it made me want to stand even closer to him. We got in the car together and started driving back to my place, both of us chatting about our work days and making small talk in general. But I couldn't shake the feeling of intense desire I felt for him. My orgasm in the showers had done little to slake my lust for Tyler. It was never-ending. Every moment we spent together, all I could think about was jumping his bones. As he talked a little shop, I kept imagining the two of us groping and kissing in the car, what it would feel like for him to lean over that center console and give me head. Maybe parked at lover's lane. Or anywhere, really.

I was swiftly discovering that it didn't matter where, when, why, or how—I was always ravenous for Tyler's body. I needed him, and that desire wasn't going anywhere anytime soon.

TYLER

By the time we got back to Mason's house, my heart was racing. I had gotten so caught up in the day that everything else seemed to fade to the background when the two of us were together. It seemed inevitable, even when we were being productive and working out. All my problems seemed to melt away when Mason was at my side, and judging by how enthusiastic he was, he felt the same about my company. Or at least, that was what I wanted to think. I was a chronic overthinker.

I had barely been able to contain myself in the shower earlier. After a day of teasing me the way he had been, it had been hard to focus. I had wanted to lock whatever doors could have given us some privacy in the shower and let loose all the cravings I had in those few steamy minutes we spent together. We'd been able to stay focused on working out and getting in shape for the game up until then, but something about Mason kept getting back into my head and distracting me.

"So," I said as we strode through the front door of Mason's house, gym bags over our shoulders, "I wanted to save it for as long as I could, but I don't think I can hold it in anymore: I've got good news on your truck."

Mason whipped around as if struck by lightning, and his face lit up just as much.

"You're kidding!" he said with that smile that set my heart racing. "Already? I knew you were backed up, so I figured it would be a while."

"Well, it'll be a bit before I get a chance to actually work on it," I admitted sheepishly, "but I tracked down a few of the parts I'll need, and I still want to take a second look at it soon and make sure I'm not missing anything, but if I'm not...I feel good saying I reckon I can have her fixed up in about a month."

Mason dropped his bag on the ground, and he lurched forward toward me so fast my instincts told me he was about to tackle me to the ground. And honestly, I would have been just fine with that. But to my surprise, he wrapped his arms around my waist, scooped me up into the air as if I was weightless, and spun me around while I held on to his shoulders and laughed. My cheeks were blushing intensely, and I couldn't help but laugh as he whirled me around and set me back down, dizzy and flustered.

"That's incredible, man!" he said, grinning from ear to ear. "Do I even want to ask how you were able to find the parts you need? Can I pay you anything more?"

"No and no," I insisted, still trying to keep myself from laughing. "I won't bother you with the details for now, but it was just a matter of pulling some strings. And what you're doing for me here is more than plenty, seriously. It's only been a week, but I feel like I'm already noticing a difference," I admitted.

And that much was true. I might not have looked all that different than I did the first night I saw Mason's truck get towed to the garage, but I felt a hell of a lot better. My body seemed to have been craving some routine all along, especially one that gives it the nourishment and activity it hadn't had in a while. I woke up more easily in the mornings, fell asleep faster, and I felt like I had more energy throughout the day. It was a subtle difference, but it was there. There was no question about that.

"You should be proud of yourself, man," Mason said, putting a hand on my shoulder and giving it an affectionate squeeze. "You've put a lot of hard work into a short time. We're gonna kick ass out there on the field. But how are you feeling about the repairs? You're sure it's not more trouble than it's worth?" he asked, furrowing his brow.

"You know I do this for a living, right?" I retorted with a wink. "You kind of gave me a dream project to work on."

"I could say the same thing," he said, chuckling, and he left me to stew on that with wide eyes as he moved past me to go into the kitchen. "But for now, I think we have cause to celebrate."

"Celebrate?" I asked, following him in.

He made his way to a small but well-stocked wine rack, putting his fist to his mouth and giving a thoughtful hum as he perused his selection.

"Are you more of a sweet or dry type?" he asked.

"I think that's for you to decide," I said, unable to resist myself. "You're the one who's been assessing me all week, after all."

He looked over his shoulder at me with that almost roguish grin that I fell for every time.

"In that case, I think a nice Shiraz with cherry undertones would be good. How does that sound?" he asked, pulling a bottle from the shelf and carrying it over to the counter to uncork.

He stuck the corkscrew into the top and gripped the top of it with a large, muscular hand, and with only a couple of firm, powerful twists, he had drilled the thing all the way down into the bottle. With a pop, the cork came out, making the whole bottle look downright delicate in his grip. I had gotten so wrapped up staring at the simple task that it took me an extra moment to think of a response. And I frankly had no idea whether Shiraz was a flirty answer, so I made a mental note to look up wines later. For now, I'd just play it by ear.

"Th-that sounds great." I chuckled, rubbing the back of my neck. "I hear red wine is good for you, right?"

"Well, that answer changes every few years, it feels like," he said. "But in general, I don't think there's a doctor in the world who would fault you for a glass of red a night."

"If only they could say the same thing about burgers," I sighed, joking, and Mason laughed while beckoning me over to the glasses he was setting out.

He poured us sizeable glasses, more sizeable than I would have expected from a celebration, but it was certainly late enough to warrant it. I sure wasn't going to complain.

"Unfortunately, burgers are not on the menu tonight, but I have another one I was saving for a day where we'd be feeling creative," he said, narrowing his eyes.

Before I could respond, he held up his glass to mine, and I clinked it to his.

"Creative?" I asked, raising my eyebrows before we took our first sips. "Oh my god, this is delicious. But, uh, I don't know how I should feel about the word 'creative' when I don't think I have a strong grasp of normal cooking."

"Aha, there's the difference," Mason said. "This isn't *cooking*, if you want to get technical about it. And I know how you like getting technical."

"You could say I err on technical," I said with a laugh.

"Then you'll love this," Mason said, clapping his hands and rubbing them enthusiastically. "Sushi."

"Sushi?" I repeated, perplexed.

"I know what you're thinking," he said as he started taking out a couple of cutting boards and moving between the fridge and the counter, transporting vegetables. "It's an odd choice. I think you'd hit Charleston before you found any sushi places around here unless you're picking some up at a grocery store. And they're usually in too much of a hurry to get it *right*," he said, making a circle with his fingers as he turned to gesture to me while he spoke.

He was such an animated person that every time he got to talking about something that excited him, that passion came through.

"Don't know if I've ever had sushi, now that you mention it," I admitted.

"The most important thing is to make sure everything you use is fresh," he explained. "Come over by me and grab a knife. I'll show you."

Ingredient by ingredient, Mason walked me through making sushi, the last thing I'd expected to learn how to make tonight. Making the sticky rice was easy, but the whole process turned out to be a hell of a lot more straightforward than I had been expecting... even though I was sure my technique left a little to be desired. We were starting simple, and Mason wanted me to get introduced to sushi with something that was a little easier for a guy like me to appreciate: a Seattle roll.

We cut up avocado and cucumber into long, thin slices and set aside the sticky rice and fish roe. I stood at Mason's side as he prepared the raw salmon. Before long, I was looking at a bamboo rolling mat topped with a square of dry seaweed, with the sticky white rice and all the other ingredients we had prepped.

"This is gonna sound pretty damn unrefined of me to say," I admitted, looking down at what would soon be sushi rolls, "but it's kinda cool to see when it actually starts to look like sushi."

"That's not dumb," Mason said with a laugh. "But we're not quite there yet. Here, you need to roll it. I'll guide you through the first one. Then you do the second one."

Before I could reply, he stepped up behind me and took my hands in his as his front pressed against me and his head hovered over my shoulder. I felt my whole body warm against him, and I felt more nervous than I had when I was slicing the cucumber. He guided my fingers with a firm but gentle grip to the bottom of the seaweed.

"You want to keep it all nice and tight," he said over my shoulder in a low, husky tone that sent a shiver down my back. "That's what makes it look good and professional."

"Like this?" I asked, trying to take a little more control over my motions, to test my limits, but I was pleased to find that he squeezed my hands and guided me more firmly, almost taking over the movements of my hands.

"Just like that," he murmured. "Now cut that into eight slices, and we're in business."

I did as he said, repeated the second roll without assistance, and we soon had a platter full of what I had to admit were pretty appetizing pieces of sushi. We adorned them with a sprinkling of fish roe, and to my surprise, Mason already had a little ginger and wasabi on hand.

"There you have it," Mason was saying. "And it's not just a healthy meal for weight loss, since that's not all we're going for. It's low cholesterol too, which is something a high-fat and high-sodium diet makes you want to keep an eye on. And fish is one of the healthiest things you can eat. You don't want to slack on that protein, either, which is why there's a *little* more salmon in this than you'd probably see in a restaurant. And now you know how to make sushi," he declared, smiling proudly at me.

"Well, shit, I do, don't I?" I laughed, and Mason raised a glass to me before we drained them.

Time had flown while we cooked, and I was feeling a little looser thanks to the wine. We sat down at the kitchen table and ate the dinner we'd made while I went over the details of what the truck needed specifically. Mason listened attentively, hanging on to every word coming out of my mouth. Even he was impressed with my prediction that I'd be able to get her running again, after he heard the multiple issues with it, but that only made his mood brighter.

"I've gotta say," Mason said after he finished his last bite of sushi, "the things you're able to do in that garage sound like magic sometimes. Didn't I hear through the grapevine one time that Mr. Carmichael tried to let you take Shop class twice?"

"You bet your ass you did," I said, brightening up and leaning forward across the table. "No, you don't get it, it's complete bullshit they didn't let us do that. We had this whole plan sketched out where it was going to work around my football schedule like an after-school program."

"You *actually* tried to take Shop twice?" Mason laughed, his cheeks as rosy from the wine as my own were.

"Shut up!" I laughed, sitting back. "I bet you would have taken gym as a directed study if they'd let you."

"Well, you got me there, but that's what they had sports teams for," Mason said with a grin.

"I know, and I bet that's why my plans got blocked," I said, wagging a conspiratorial finger and raising my eyebrows. "Coach probably got wind of it and thought it would make it hard for me to focus on the team."

"Would it have?" he asked.

I opened and closed my mouth a few times, trying to think of an honest answer, but Mason's spreading grin told me I was caught.

"Yeah," I confessed, and Mason clucked his tongue.

"You would have left me all alone out there on the field?" he playfully protested, and I felt his leg bump against mine under the table.

"I bet I could have tempted you to after-school Shop," I said, giving him a smug smirk. "We could have spent those long afternoons bent over whatever junker Mr. Carmichael could get a hold of, maybe build some parts of a few tackling dummies for the football team."

"I bet you could have," Mason said, and I realized he was staring far too deep into my eyes across the table, with that faint but potent smile that made me feel like that bottle of wine he had pulled open with such ease. "See, if we'd been closer back in high school I think we would have been a power couple."

"Not if I'd bored you to death talkin' about whatever books I had been reading." I chuckled.

"I dunno, fixing up a car over an afternoon talking about a good book sounds like a pretty ideal day, if you ask me," he said.

When I didn't respond, a tense silence fell between us for a moment. There was so much racing through my mind that I didn't know what to get out first. There was no question on my mind I wanted more with Mason. I wanted to spend afternoons shooting the breeze with him and feeling his warmth in bed at night, see what he was like on a regular day, really get to know each other the way both of us seemed to feel so hungry for.

"But here, we should get the kitchen cleaned up," Mason said suddenly, and I realized I had let the moment last too long.

Relatively quietly, we got the dishes washed and the kitchen

96

looking spotless. That was part of Mason's routine, he had said at the start of the week. Cleaning up as you went kept you busy, and it was good for your mental health. A clean house helped calm you down and keep your stress that much more manageable. I had always known that a clean room helped me sleep at night, but it was all too easy to let a messy house get away from you.

"I'll catch you in the morning. I need to sketch up next week's meal plan," Mason said once we finished, and I could have sworn there was something off about the smile on his face. "See you bright and early?"

"You know it," I said, grinning. "And hey, thanks. Let's do sushi again soon."

He nodded, and we went our separate ways, him to the master bedroom and me to the guest room. The room I had settled into was nicer than I had been expecting. Mason rented this place, and like a lot of real estate in the country where few people lived, everything about it was a little bigger and a little nicer than the houses in a larger town. This room featured lovingly cared-for hardwood floors, a sturdy bed, a gorgeous window with a view of the front yard and sunrise, and just enough storage for anything I wanted to keep with me. It had taken me all of a few hours to get my things together to move in, and honestly, it had felt so natural that I already felt it was going to be strange moving back into my parents' house.

That thought wasn't pleasant. I loved my parents, but frankly, I felt like I had been walking on clouds since *meeting* Mason, much more so from living with him. Sleeping was going to be difficult tonight. It wouldn't be the first time. Hell, how could I sleep when Mason was just a few feet down the hallway from me? Just the thought of him sleeping in that massive bed – bare limbs sprawled out as his chest rose and fell in the darkness – had me feeling itchy.

I sat down on my bed and stripped off my clothes, then changed into a shirt and sleeping pants, but the hardness between my legs proved inconvenient. *That* was precisely why sleeping was going to be tough tonight.

But what was I going to do about it? Get up, storm down the hallway, knock on Mason's door, tell him how I felt, and kiss those full, pink lips so hard they went red? No, of course I wasn't going to do that.

The next moment, I contradicted that thought by getting up out of bed and crossing the room to go do just that. I put my hand on the doorknob, turned it, and pulled it open.

Mason froze, inches from my door, fist raised to knock and eyes wide.

MASON

I COULD HARDLY BELIEVE THE GLORIOUS SIGHT BEFORE MY EYES.

God, he looked so damn delicious standing there in the doorway in front of me. I had come trawling down the hallway almost in a trace, unable to keep my feet from carrying me closer and closer to him, as though guided by some ghostly hand, some undeniable instinctual need to be near him. I had known from the second I'd crawled into bed and my cheek had touched the pillow that there was no use trying to fight the urge, the adrenaline pumping intoxicating endorphins of desire through my veins. No amount of self-control or internal coaching could talk me out of my feelings for Tyler. He was everything I had ever hoped for, everything I had never known I could find in this world. How could I have known that within the city limits of this tiny, rural, tight-knit community of Winchester I could run into the perfect man? I had been aching for him the first moment we were reunited at the garage, when he had appeared out of the shadows like some Herculean hero.

I had done everything I could think of to resist him. I had worked out my body, thinking that if I burned off that extra energy, there would be nothing left to pour into my emotions, my pulsing desire for him. I had thought my little self-love session in the gym showers earlier would slake my thirst. I had thought going to bed in a separate room would do the trick. But as it turned out, there was nothing I could do to keep me from ending up right here, riveted to the spot, standing in front of this adorably sexy man.

His hair was slightly tousled and messy, like he had been anxiously raking his fingers through it while pacing back and forth in the guest room. There was a look of finality on his face, a resignation mingled with excitement that made my loins stir. He was wearing nothing but a T-shirt and soft, fleece sweatpants. They were heather gray and looked well-worn and cozy, like he had been wearing them for years now. They so perfectly hugged his body, showing off those muscular thighs and calves, as well as the best part of all: his clearly outlined bulge stiffening at the front of his sweatpants. I licked my lips, following the shape of that bulge. His cock was massive and slightly twitching under the soft fabric of the sweatpants. It took all my willpower not to just immediately cup that bulge in my hand. I ached for it, every cell in my body longing to touch him, to grope him, to feel up every glorious inch of his powerful frame.

Especially because I knew he would let me do it. Willingly. Gladly. The expression on his handsome, endearing face told me everything. Those perfect, plush lips were slightly parted, his chest heaving as he breathed raggedly, desire clouding his sense of reason. His cheeks were faintly flushed, like he was both riled up and slightly embarrassed at the same time. That only served to turn me on even more as I felt the effect I was having on him. It was a thrill to realize that I could excite and entice him the same way he excited and enticed me. His perfectly smooth skin was rosy with lust, that faint shadow of stubble along his jaw adding a sense of rugged manliness to his otherwise sweet, guileless face.

He was almost as youthful looking now as he had been when we were just two quiet guys on the football team, running drills after school. There were moments in which I glanced at him and saw that same boy, that seventeen-year-old Tyler who had been so stoic and tall and quietly powerful. I remembered the way he used to dash up the field, tackling our opponents to the green turf. He had been a damn legend back then. Coach had treated him like a brick wall. He had known he could put Tyler in the game and prevent the opposing team from ever making it to the end of the field. He had been so good at the position he played, so perfectly suited to the linebacker archetype. And yet, he was a gentle giant. He was soft-spoken and thoughtful and kind. He carried a weighty sort of grace and peace that had impressed me then as much as it did now. Flat out, Tyler was gorgeous, mind, body, and soul.

God, those eyes... heavily lidded and faintly luminous in the low, glowing light of the vintage sconce on the hallway wall behind me. He looked every bit like some sexy model from a calendar shoot, designed specifically to cater to my exact tastes. Tyler was putting off an energy that made me tighten and clench at my very core, my whole body itching to press up against his. I wanted him. Desperately and unabashedly. Any shame or guilt or trepidation had flown straight out the window the second he opened the door and found me standing here with my hand raised, hovering and poised to knock. Any hesitation I might have felt before had disintegrated as soon as I realized we were not only on the same page, but also on the same paragraph, the same sentence.

And it was most certainly an exclamation, judging by the sheer magnetic attraction crackling between us like a fallen power line. I was frozen in place, overwhelmed and bowled over by how desperately I wanted him. I had felt lust before, of course. I was an adult man, after all. Plus, I worked at a gym. I had seen all kinds of handsome, incredibly fit men working their bodies to the limit. But nobody turned me on quite like Tyler. I couldn't exactly put my finger on it, but I knew what I felt for him was different somehow. It was more powerful. It was inevitable. And perhaps most importantly of all, it seemed to be reciprocal.

"Hey," I said softly, unable to think of anything to say that would contain the magnitude of my emotions.

"Hi," Tyler replied, his voice muted but slightly breathless.

"I, uh, I couldn't sleep," I told him, as if that wasn't glaringly obvious already.

I was at a total loss for anything else to say. It almost felt as though we had moved beyond mere words. There was something more primal going on between us, something without a name but utterly in control of both of us.

"Me neither," he said. "You'd think I would be exhausted after the day I've had, but... I just feel like I've got this crazy energy running through my veins. I-I don't understand it."

"I feel the same way," I agreed.

"I got in bed and lay down and tried to close my eyes, but all I could think about was how close you were, how you were just down the hallway. Just barely beyond my reach," he said, furrowing his dark brows.

"I don't think I could have escaped this, even if I had managed to fall asleep. I'm one hundred percent sure I would just run into you again in my dreams. You're always on my mind lately, Tyler, and I can't seem to shake you," I admitted.

"I can't stop thinkin' about you either," he said, taking half a step closer.

I felt my body instantly respond to this subtle movement, my heart skipping a beat or two. I softly inhaled, breathing in his delicious, heady scent. I longed to bury my face in his neck, run my fingers through his thick, fluffy hair, press the hard length of my body against his.

"What a crazy predicament we've found ourselves in here," I sighed, shaking my head.

Tyler laughed softly, scratching at the back of his head. A soft flush spread across his cheeks, and I bit my lip. God, I wanted to kiss him so badly. It required all my self-control and strength to stand here, totally still, while I resisted the urge to throw my arms around this gorgeous beast of a man.

"I didn't think... I just didn't see it coming," I said. "But I should have. Because goddamn, Tyler, you're so fine. You've got me hooked, man, and there's no goin' back."

"Then don't resist. Don't hold back. I promise, whatever you have in store for me, I can take it. Gladly. Willingly. I want you, Mace. I know it's unprofessional. I know it's probably not the smartest idea in the world, but I can't deny it any longer. My feelings for you clearly aren't going away anytime soon," he explained.

"Then what on earth are we waiting for?" I murmured.

I took a step closer, shortening the distance between us. Tyler's eyes widened, and he began to breathe more heavily. I saw his cock stiffening at the front of his sweatpants, and I couldn't resist any longer. I closed the space between us and cupped his face in my hands, diving in for a passionate kiss. He moaned against my mouth as our lips parted, my tongue probing into his warm, wet mouth. I pushed my way into the guest room, fumbling to shut the door behind me. I grabbed Tyler by the shoulders and spun him around, pinning him to the wall as I rutted into him, my cock getting rock hard as his shaft slid up and down along my thigh. I groaned and nipped playfully at his bottom lip, making him gasp. His cock twitched against my leg, making me press into him even harder. His hands reached up first to cup my face, then slid down my neck, my shoulders, down my arms. He rocked gently back and forth on the balls of his feet, letting his hard cock create friction against my leg. I groaned in appreciation, reaching up to tangle my fingers in his hair to hold him there. He wasn't going anywhere. Not as long as I was in charge.

"God, I should have known this would happen," Tyler managed to choke out as we broke apart for a moment for air. "I've wanted you ever since we were in high school, Mason. I used to watch you running drills on the football field and think about how you would look naked. I touched myself in the showers. I thought about you when I got hard."

"I feel the same way about you," I growled. "I've always been hot for you, Tyler. I can't believe I'm finally getting to touch you like this after all those years."

"Then don't hold back. I want you. All of you. And I'm not afraid of what might happen. I just want you to do whatever you want with me," he hissed. "Make me yours. Claim me."

"Oh, I absolutely intend to," I snarled with a devilish grin.

I let my hand slip down his body, caressing his hips and pelvic vee down to the bulge between his thighs. He let out a soft, dreamy sigh as I cupped his thick cock. I licked my lips in anticipation, massaging his hardness through the soft fabric of his sweatpants. He groaned and pressed into my hand, melting into my touch with pure need. I kissed him harder this time, rocking my hips so that his cock and mine slid up and down against each other, still confined by our lounge pants. I could tell he wasn't wearing boxers or briefs underneath, and that gave me a little thrill. My lips trailed down from his lips along his stubbly, rough jaw and down the side of his ticklish neck. He shivered and groaned with pleasure as I breathed gently over the shell of his ear, my teeth softly grazing the smooth, sensitive flesh there. I nibbled his earlobe while we rutted against each other, my cock twitching at Tyler's every gasp and moan.

I could hardly wait to get our clothes off, but at the same time, there was something undeniably delicious about postponing our pleasure, frotting together like two hormonal teenagers. And what else were we, really, at our core? Being around Tyler made me feel like a man and a gawky teen at the same time. But now we were adults, and there was no question. There was no barrier keeping us from doing exactly what we wanted to do. Was it professional? No. Was it casual? Hell no. But was any of that going to stop me? Absolutely not. We were hurtling toward the same incredible burst of desire, and there was no going back now. Not that I even wanted to.

I tugged at the bottom of his T-shirt, hinting at what I wanted from him. Tyler lifted his strong arms over his head, and I yanked the shirt up, pulling it off and tossing it aside to bare his powerful chest. My hands roved up and down his torso, clawing softly at his broad back, feeling the raw muscle rippling under his skin. I followed down his neck to his collarbone and chest, kissing and biting lightly, sucking at his soft skin to leave deep purplish-red love bruises to claim him as mine. I wanted him to look in the mirror later and see those marks. I wanted him to carry a temporary reminder of what we did together, of who he belonged to. Tyler groaned and whimpered under my touch, making my cock twitch for more.

"Take off your pants," I growled in his ear.

He hastily followed my command, pulling down his sweatpants and kicking them off to the side so that his cock sprang free into the cool air. I groaned my appreciation and wrapped a hand around his shaft, sliding up and down loosely until he was panting and moaning. Then I pulled off my shirt and pants. We were naked and pressed up against one another at the wall. To my amazement, Tyler dropped to his knees in front of me, those gorgeous eyes glancing up with a silent question in them. With my lips parted and my heart pounding like mad, I could only give him a curt nod of approval. Words failed me when I looked at him, kneeling before me and ready to give me so much pleasure.

I inhaled sharply as he sucked the head of my cock between his lips. He wrapped one large hand around my thick, stiff cock and began to pump me in tandem with his hot, wet mouth. His tongue lathed along the sensitive underside of my shaft, and I trembled with bliss, reaching out both arms to brace myself against the wall while Tyler sucked my cock greedily. I glanced down to see him bobbing up and down on my rod, slurping and sucking like he was beyond desperate for my taste. I nearly lost control when I noticed he was stroking himself at the same time, pleasuring himself while he sucked me off.

"Fuck, that feels so good," I murmured raggedly.

"Mmm," Tyler moaned, sending delicious vibrations up through my pelvis.

"I can't wait to fuck you hard," I growled.

Tyler glanced up at me with my cock still in his mouth, his eyes wide and round with desire. He looked so damn gorgeous like that I wished I could freeze-frame that image in my mind, frame it so I could reflect on this glorious moment forever. He was beautiful, and he was all mine for the taking.

He sucked harder and deeper, taking my cock down inch by inch until I could feel the tip of my cock brushing against the back of his throat. To my awe, he didn't choke. He started to cough for a second, then quickly recovered, his tongue swirling around the thick root of my shaft. I was starting to lose control, my hips rolling back and forth as I almost fucked his face. His mouth was so perfectly divine, warm and inviting, his tongue doing expert work. I didn't want to stop him, but I also knew that if I let this go on for too much longer, I would not be able to hold back. I didn't want to roll past the point of no return. Not yet. I still had so much I wanted to do with him. To him. Inside him.

So before he could suck me all the way to the edge, I gently pushed him back. My cock slipped out of his mouth with a wet pop, and he licked his lips, looking up at me questioningly. I gave him a filthy grin and gestured for him to stand up, which he obeyed gladly.

"Come on," I said in a rough, needy voice. "Come to bed."

TYLER

MASON TOOK MY HAND IN HIS, AND HE LED ME OUT OF THE ROOM AND down the hall before I had time to even fully process what was happening. I was still swimming in the foggy warmth of having my lips wrapped around Mason's cock and tasting every inch of it that I could get my mouth on. The day had been full of so much that my senses were totally overwhelmed, and in that moment, everything happening between Mason and me pushed everything else to the side. There was nothing but us and what we were doing with our bodies.

I had expected the tension to burst the moment our lips met, but if I was being honest, I was only feeling more wound up. I felt like a guitar tuned too tight, desperate to be plucked by the overwhelming, powerful man leading me by the hand down the hall and into the master bedroom.

The room was so much like what I had pictured in my head that it gave me chills. I had seen Mason's room before and appreciated his very clean, minimalist tastes, but it was the scene I could see played out that got my blood running hotter. His clothes were tossed haphazardly on the footboard, as if he'd been as pent up and frustrated as I had. The pillows on the massive bed were a little askew, as if he'd been tossing and turning for a few moments, and the sheets were thrown back in a hurry. I could practically see Mason in my imagination, dealing with the same tension as I was until he couldn't take it anymore, tossed the covers off, and stormed down the hall to claim me.

Claiming me. That was a thought that sent shivers down my spine in all the best ways, and I knew that was happening. He had me in his house, now in his bedroom, and in a matter of seconds, I would be on that bed.

As soon as we were at the bed, Mason tightened his grip on my hand and playfully swung me around onto it, sending me sprawling on the still warm sheets as I landed on my back and pushed myself toward the center of the mattress. Mason loomed over me with that wicked, sinful smile on his face. His hand wrapped around his cock, which was still glistening from all the attention I had been giving it just moments ago. Mason's cheeks were pink, and his eyes were full of hunger for me as he knelt on the bed, still stroking his cock.

He was on me faster than I could react. He bent down over me, and I wrapped my legs around his waist as he cupped my face in his hands and kissed me hard. He took my lower lip in between his teeth and worried it as his hands went behind my back. He dragged his nails down my body, and I felt his shaft growing tauter and harder by the second.

It pressed against mine, our swords crossed at the bases, and I felt the soft but forceful pulse of his cock as he ground his hips into mine. We were so vulnerable together, which made it all the stranger that when I was in Mason's arms, I felt more powerful than ever.

The feelings overwhelmed me at the same time that he took his time exploring my body with those strong hands and fingers. Mason was a dominant man. I didn't think there was anyone who could challenge that simple fact. He got people to improve themselves by being a hard-ass instructor in many ways, including with me. Hell, there were some points in our training together that I became frustrated, wanted to tell the football players to fuck off, and throw in the towel. But it was Mason's encouragement that kept me going, and it was the desire to see in myself what he saw in me that made it impossible to chicken out.

Mason was exactly the force I needed in my life, and he wasn't just willing; he was eager.

He broke the kiss long enough to work his way to my side and get an arm under my thigh. His greedy hand found my ass, and it pinched my cheeks before slipping a finger to my tight hole. I couldn't stop myself from groaning as that wandering finger explored me, finding its way around in a slow circle until it was comfortable enough to start teasing me. Finally, he slid it in, and he brought his mouth to my neck.

My rigid manhood bobbed softly against my stomach as Mason took his time fingering me. I felt Mason's smiling mouth on my neck, and even as I squirmed away as much as his grip would let me, he just seemed to enjoy it even more. He adored every twitch and groan he got out of me, and he knew exactly how flustered and exposed it made me feel. I was in good hands, and I wouldn't feel okay doing any of this with anyone but Mason, but god, Mason knew how to do it just right.

I reached down to my cock and started massaging it with my hand while Mason had his preoccupied. Warm waves of pleasure rolled up my body, even though this was all a tease. Just as I thought, it didn't take long before Mason couldn't hold himself back anymore.

He slipped his fingers out of my hole and crawled to the bedside table, where he took out a condom and put it on. Once he had done the same with lube, he approached me again with that ravenous look on his face.

"Still with me?" he purred, running his hand through my hair and looking down at me lovingly. "I want you to enjoy this every bit as much as I'm about to."

"Man," I breathed, "that's going to be tough because I was about to ask you the same thing."

"Good," he growled.

He pushed my legs as far back as they would go, and he slipped the tip of his crown into my hole. That bulging head pushed into me, and immediately, that warmth that was spreading through my body felt many, many times more fulfilling. I didn't just feel good. I felt safe with Mason, and that made his entry all the sweeter. The shower had been hot, passionate, and impulsive. It had been unbelievably good, so much so that I could still barely believe that happened. But this still felt somehow...different. Maybe it was the emotions crackling through the air like lightning between us, or maybe it was just the simple fact that living together made us even more unable to resist each other.

I didn't care to think about it too much, and possibly for the first time in my life, that felt like one massive relief.

Mason slid further into me, inch by inch, making sure that my body was ready to receive him with each gentle thrust of his hips. I couldn't have asked for someone more considerate and patient with me, in bed and out. He started rocking back and forth, faster, and I let my head fall and to the side. My eyes caught sight of a mirror on the wall, where I got a full view of Mason's perfectly sculpted body claiming mine.

My first instinct was to feel self-conscious because my body wasn't quite where I was happy with it yet. But the more I watched Mason groping me, the more I saw that sincere, overwhelming desire in his eyes that didn't care about how much extra there was on my body, I found it easier to push that insecurity away. Within seconds, it was gone, burned away by the heat I felt from the sight of Mason rutting into me faster and faster.

I turned my head back up to lock gazes with Mason, and my heart skipped a beat as he smiled. He was panting as he fucked me, and there was something so open and shameless about it that made me feel nothing but sweet, emotional release.

Physical release was not far behind it, either. Mason's rhythm was unstoppable, and he reached down to wrap his hand around my shaft. I felt his grip moving across the length of my cock, and I had to grip the sheets to keep it together. Mason didn't just make me feel what I wanted to feel. He could take me to the heights *he* wanted me to feel, and beyond. Every time he slid in and out, I felt every inch of that thick cock pushing into me and filling me with warmth. My whole body felt warmer and looser despite my muscles around my groin feeling tighter, spooling up and begging to be let go.

Mason's hand made my shaft pulse and throb, and I felt wetness spreading over it as I released a little precome that got lost in the mess of Mason's hand and its steady work. The fire within it felt white hot, and everything felt so taut and desperate for release that I felt like I could have been tipped over and poured myself out.

That was when I became aware that Mason's balls were clenching, and he did the same to his jaw, sucking in a sharp hiss of air before he bent down and kissed me. My hands reached up to hug him closer, and in one great burst, we came together, lips locked and eyes clenched shut as Mason guided me through my orgasm. I felt myself pulsing in time with him as we released everything we had, and bit by bit, the tension melted away, taking all the worries and stresses of the day with it.

When it was over, my whole body felt like a useless mess, and I couldn't stop from smiling. Mason kept our kiss going, though, and it felt like we were together for an eternity before he pushed himself up and smile down at me.

"God, you look hot in the afterglow," he murmured, running a thumb over my lip.

"You're one to talk," I whispered.

We got ourselves cleaned up, but without warning, all the exertion of the day decided this was an ideal time to catch up to me. Mason seemed to feel the same. Minutes after we were washed up, we simply melted back into bed.

The sounds of crickets outside were more than enough background noise to lull us to sleep as we worked our nude bodies into the fresh, clean sheets and blankets, and as soon as I felt his strong arms wrapping around me, I was out like a light.

* * *

WHEN I OPENED my eyes the next morning, the first thing I saw at my side was an empty bed with the sheets disturbed.

Waking up came as a surprise to me. It was the kind of sudden, heavy sleep that made me forget any time had actually passed, as if I just blinked and it was suddenly bright out. The room was remarkably still and peaceful, and the faint ringing in my ears was the only sound that reached me for those first few, sleepy minutes. But that didn't last long.

Mason had taught me that getting up as soon as I was awake was the better way to do things, no matter how tempting it was to wallow in the indulgent caress of soft and warm sheets. Lying in bed for longer was a surefire way to keep you groggy or make you fall right back asleep, and that threw off your body's natural rhythms. And I had to admit that as I stood up and stretched my nude body out, feeling all my muscles coming awake slowly, it felt better.

I padded into the en suite bathroom, wondering where Mason had gone off to. I didn't have any worries at first that he had run off last night after I fell asleep. This was his house, after all, so there wasn't anywhere to go. Well, that nice thought lasted a few moments before I started to feel that twinge of familiar anxiety. We hadn't rushed things too much last night, had we? Mason had been right there at my bedroom door, waiting for it to happen, egging it along, meeting me halfway. Of course, what a man did in the heat of the moment wasn't nearly as important as what he did after that had passed.

I went into the bathroom and caught sight of my naked body, and I paused. A faint smile crossed my lips as I turned, looking at myself in the mirror, and I had to admit I felt my heart rate pick up in a good way. I had to remind myself that I was always slimmer in the morning, but when I flexed, the shape of my arms looked a little more defined to me. I ran my hands over my stomach and love handles, and while it certainly wasn't the kind of difference I could put into a *Before and After* comparison, it was there.

A minute later, when I walked out of the bedroom in the clothes I'd meant to sleep in, my questions were answered in the form of an aroma so welcoming and delicious that I felt like I could have floated and followed it all the way to the kitchen. I appeared in the doorway to see Mason standing at the stove, and I approached him just in time to watch him stirring what looked like-

"Scrambled egg whites, spinach, tomato, yellow peppers, crumbled turkey bacon, and as many spices as I could get my hands on," Mason said before I could even open my mouth, and he turned to smile at me with a freshly shaven face and well-rested eyes.

I couldn't believe the guy. Even first thing in the morning, that glow he seemed to have on him just never went away, did it? I wanted to hug him from behind and kiss his neck for being so thoughtful as to get up and start making us breakfast, but I wasn't sure whether or not we were on the same page about everything that had happened last night. I opened my mouth to say as much, but before a word could escape my mouth, Mason answered it for me.

He leaned in and gave me a quick peck on the cheek. Such a simple gesture that held so many words.

"Sleep well?" he asked.

I was at a loss for an answer for a few moments, and I almost laughed.

"Yeah," I finally admitted. "Really well, actually. Barely feels like any time passed."

"Good, glad it's not just me." He chuckled. "This'll be ready in a few. If you want to make some coffee, the coffee maker is all ready to go. I just haven't started it yet."

While Mason finished making a healthy breakfast, I set to making us some coffee, but after only a few moments, I felt the irresistible urge to bring up that sensitive topic.

"So, hey, about last night," I said, with all the tact of an elephant bull in a china shop.

"Did you enjoy it?" he asked, raising a concerned eyebrow.

I was stunned to silence for a moment, and I had to laugh, blushing

as I pushed the button to start the coffee drip and turned to face him again.

"I – I mean, yeah!" I admitted. "It was incredible. *You're* incredible. I mean, I don't want to sound like – damn, I probably shouldn't have tried to get my thoughts in order before coffee," I joked, trying to play off my faux pas casually, but Mason seemed to be having none of it.

Having just finished the eggs, he quickly served a couple of plates full of it, then set down the spatula and approached me. He wrapped one hand around the back of my head and the other around my half-hard cock, and he used both to draw me close to him and press a kiss to my lips. He tasted like the breakfast we were about to eat, and the smell of coffee behind me filled my nose as I felt his warm hand massage my manhood. The kiss seemed to silence the room, and I couldn't hold back a quiet groan as I felt myself pulse in his hand.

"How does that work for putting your thoughts in order?" Mason said in that husky tone that made me hungry for more than just eggs. "I don't regret anything I said last night, if that's what you mean."

"Good," I breathed, relieved. "Me either. This is just a lot to happen so fast."

"You're right about that," Mason admitted, heading back to the plates and picking them both up.

The visual of a shirtless Mason wearing nothing but sleeping shorts and standing there with two plates heavy with food was a treat I hadn't known I needed in my life so badly. It was almost enough to make me forget that I was so worked up in the first place.

"I just didn't want you to think this was some...stupid ploy to get close to you, if that makes sense," I said at last, and it felt like a massive weight off my shoulders. "I like you, I like what's happening here, and I don't mind that it's going fast. I just don't want to be misunderstood."

"I appreciate you being up front about that," Mason said, approaching me with a warm smile on his face. "But don't worry, I don't have any sneaking suspicions that you're anyone but a sweet, hot man who deserves good things in life. And I don't know how good this fry-up is, so I think we should be the judges of that," he finished with a grin.

"I think that sounds pretty great," I admitted, blushing, and I followed him to the kitchen table.

"Besides," he said as he sat down and drove a fork into his food, "this is good cardio, so don't expect me to slack off in bed anytime soon."

MASON

Two weeks had flown by so fast I barely realized we had fallen into a routine. I woke up smiling, the first pale rays of sunshine filtering through the blinds in such a way as to be nearly blinding. It wasn't quite dawn yet, as evidenced by the number glowing bright green on the nightstand alarm clock. The bedroom was cast in an unearthly glow, the shadows bluish black and the light a reddish gold. I lay there for a few moments trying to let my mind slowly come to life as I watched the shadows of tree branches sway and dance on the ceiling. The fan turned slowly, mainly for the comforting background noise than for cooler air, since it was still springtime here in Winchester, and it could be a little chilly at night. But here in my bed, snuggled underneath the sheets and fleece blankets with Tyler, I was comfortable and warm. His body put off so much heat it felt like I was sleeping next to a radiator or maybe just a gigantic space heater. Either way, it only served to make him extra cuddle-worthy on these brisk mornings. I could see the faintest crackle of frost along the windowpane, the kind that was as ephemeral as the early morning dew on the lawn. It would dissipate by the time we rolled out of bed most mornings. This was the time of year when the mornings would start out crisp and cool and then crescendo into a warm, hazy afternoon. It was always difficult to know how to dress for the day if you were going to be outside because your coat and scarf would be entirely too toasty by the time two o'clock rolled around.

I glanced sidelong at Tyler, almost letting out a laugh as I noticed his tousled, messy hair just barely poking out from under the sheets. It was the only part of his body visible at the moment. I wondered how the hell he could breathe under there. I was torn—I wanted to wake him up so we could snuggle and talk softly as we had been doing nearly every morning for the past two weeks, but then... he looked so sweet and peaceful sleeping under the blankets beside me. My fingers itched to stroke his soft, tufty hair. I wanted to kiss him on the forehead, stroke his cheek, wake him with gentle touches that would have him smiling sleepily as he opened his eyes.

I slowly turned over to let my gaze wander over every inch of him, listening intently to the rhythmic, soothing in and out of his breathing. I had never shared a bed with a cozier neighbor. He made me want to stay in bed all day, just build ourselves a blanket fort like my cousins and I used to do as kids and spend the chilly morning tucked away inside it, dreaming up imaginary worlds and going on adventures in the idyllic realm of our minds. I very gently tugged the blankets down a little to reveal more of Tyler's sleeping face. I followed the sharp triangular cut of his nose, the precious curve of his upper lip, the full pouting deliciousness of his bottom lip. I longed to kiss him awake and watch those gorgeous eyes flutter open in the soft light of morning, but he just looked so content I thought it might be cruel to wake him. I decided that if I was going to prod him out of slumber, I sure as hell had better come up with a damn good reason to do so. I wracked my brain for something good to offer him. It was a Saturday morning, and if the soft light outside my window was any indication of the day to come, it had the potential to be a perfect opportunity for some outdoorsy activities. I mulled it over in my mind, trying to figure out where we could go and what we could do. We both had the day off, which was a blessed rarity. We might as well make the most of it, I decided. I knew just the place to take him. A place so lovely, so romantic, so rewarding that it was worth interrupting Tyler's sleep to rouse him and get him out on a trail in the woods.

So I wiggled closer to him and pressed a soft, gentle kiss to his forehead. I heard him groan sleepily and his eyes cracked open just barely. I couldn't help but smile as I gazed into his face. He mirrored my smile, which immediately made my heart melt.

"Good morning, sleepyhead," I murmured under my breath.

"Mornin'," he mumbled back, stretching a little like a cat.

"How did you sleep?" I asked.

He shrugged and draped an arm over me, pulling me close so he could kiss the tip of my nose. God, he made my heart beat so fast.

"I slept good. Had some weird dreams, though. I was at the shop bent over this engine trying to fix it, but the parts kept moving around like some kind of bizarre Rubik's cube. Very frustrating." He chuckled.

"That doesn't sound very relaxing, no," I agreed. "Hopefully my truck doesn't treat you like that."

Tyler grinned. "Aw, no. Not at all. She's an angel, of course. Just like you are."

"Oh, come on, now. You flatter me too much," I said playfully. "But lucky for you, flattery will get you everywhere. What would you rather have for breakfast: eggs benedict or banana pancakes?"

"Hmmm," he mumbled, thinking it over. "If there was a way to combine them, that's what I'd want, but I have a feeling a banana-benedict hybrid doesn't quite fit into our meal plan, does it?"

"Not so much, no," I told him.

"Well, in that case, let's go with pancakes. And turkey bacon?" he asked.

I nodded and started pushing the bedsheets back down off of our bodies.

"Sure thing," I said with a wink.

I sat up and slid out of bed, immediately pulling on a pair of house slippers because the hardwood flooring was icy cold. I walked around to the other side of the bed to leave the room, but Tyler sat up and quickly grabbed my hand, pulling me back to kiss me. I laughed softly against his lips, feeling totally warm and fuzzy inside. Boy, he sure knew how to make a chilly spring morning feel cozier than a crackling fireplace.

"I'll be there in a minute," he said, releasing my hand.

"Good," I said, "because I've got big plans for us today."

With that, I padded off to the kitchen, unable to wipe the goofy smile from my face. I pulled out all the ingredients for my favorite banana pancakes recipe—oat flour, cashew milk, eggs, bananas, vanilla extract, coconut oil, cinnamon, nutmeg, baking soda, and honey. I whipped all the ingredients together and was in the process of pouring perfect circles of batter into a greased skillet when Tyler came sauntering into the kitchen to join me. His hair was still a mess, and there was a crease along his left cheek from lying on the hem of the pillowcase. He looked so adorable that he nearly distracted me away from the stove, but I held on. I remained strong. I couldn't abandon my post as batter-pourer and pancake-flipper just because the hottest, most tempting man in the world had just stepped into my kitchen.

"Oh, that smells heavenly. Can I help somehow?" he asked, mid-yawn.

"Actually, yes. Could you get the frozen strawberries and blueberries out of the freezer? Then I want you to pour about a cup of the frozen fruit into the saucepan next to me here on the stove along with a drizzle of coconut oil, a squeeze of lemon juice, and some honey. You're just making a simple berry compote to top off the pancakes," I explained.

"Yes, sir. Will do," he said, making my heart beat fast again. He did as instructed and then stood by me at the stove tending the berries. "So, what have you got planned for us today?"

"We're going on a hike," I declared brightly. "To a really lovely spot up in the woods. I don't know if you've ever been there before, but I think you'll like it. We'll be packing our wetsuits and a lunch."

"Wetsuits?" he repeated, raising an eyebrow.

I smiled. "Yep. But no more questions—I want to surprise you."

"Fair enough," Tyler replied warmly.

We finished cooking and sat down for a quick and delicious breakfast, then packed up some sandwiches, cut veggies, and hummus for lunch, and put on our coats and hiking boots. It was just barely nine in the morning when we headed out into the bright, sparkling sunny day. We climbed into his car and drove up to a trailhead few knew about up in the foothills beyond Lake Wren. Once we'd parked, we got started on the hike in high spirits.

"Perfect day for a hike, isn't it?" Tyler said with a smile.

He looked positively glowing with the bright sun shining on his face. All around us we could hear the playful twitterings of birds, the echoes of traffic and industry far behind us. Out here, it was easy enough to forget about the world and just exist. I had always adored the forest for that reason. There was no one around to judge me or look at me funny. The trees placed no demands on me. The forest was content to just let me be.

"Yeah, it's fantastic," I agreed.

"So, where are we going? What's the surprise?" he pressed as we hiked up the trail.

I laughed. "If I tell you now, it won't be a surprise," I said.

"Good point. I'm just impatient," he admitted.

I reached over to take his hand and give it a tight squeeze.

"Good things come to those who wait," I reminded him lightly.

"As usual, you're right," he agreed.

Although we had started out feeling a little chilly, it didn't take long for the day to start warming up. As we hiked deeper and higher up into the forest, we began to shed bits of clothing—our coats, then our scarves, then our sweaters, until we were just wearing T-shirts and sweatpants and shoes, with our extra layers packed away in our backpacks with the wetsuits and the lunch bags. It was about a two-and-a-half-hour hike up through the dense, vividly green forest until we approached the area I was most excited to show Tyler. I was starting to feel truly giddy thinking about the way he would react to the sight we were about to see.

"Oh, we're really close now," I remarked.

"Perfect. I can't wait to see what it is you're so excited about." Tyler chuckled.

"Trust me, it's totally worth the hike," I said.

"I trust you. Always," he replied meaningfully.

We walked through the dense underbrush and thick tree line, the ground underneath becoming less dirt and more smooth gray stone. We began to hear a rushing sound, and Tyler gave me a quizzical look.

"Is that... what I think it is?" he asked curiously.

"Let's find out," I teased.

We kept hiking until the rushing sound was much, much louder, and with a few more steps through the greenery, we came upon a wide-open clearing and a crystalline pool into which a tall, narrow waterfall cascaded gracefully. I watched with delight as Tyler's eyes widened and his lips mouthed the word *wow*. The waterfall stretched probably twenty or thirty feet high, slipping and raining down over the smoothed-down glossy stones of a steep, small cliff. The pool below rippled delicately, and the water was so translucent that you could see straight through to the bottom. It was quite a bit deeper than it appeared, and the water was incredibly cold. But luckily we were able to change into our wetsuits and slowly wade into the clear, frigid water.

"My god, it's cold." Tyler laughed excitedly.

"You'll get used to it, I promise," I said, already down to my waist.

"It's nice to wash off all that sweat from the hike up here. I can't believe I never knew this place existed, Mace. This is absolutely gorgeous. It hardly seems real," he gushed.

"I know, right?" I agreed. "It's one of my favorite places in the whole world, and hardly anyone even knows about it."

"No wonder it's so beautiful, then; the fewer people know about it, the more pristine and natural the place gets to stay," he mused aloud.

"Exactly," I said, dunking my whole body into the water.

I burst back out gasping for air, the frigid water on my face shocking my system. It was so refreshing and cleansing, exactly what we needed after a long work week. Tyler and I spent the next couple hours swimming around and splashing each other, occasionally pausing to cling to one another and kiss in the cold water. Once we had worked up an appetite, we pulled out our packed lunches and went to town on our sandwiches and snacks, sharing a massive bottle of water between the two of us. Then, once we were full, we both stretched out languidly on a giant, flat boulder to sun ourselves dry before starting the hike back down.

The sun was slipping closer to the horizon, no longer beating straight overhead. Tyler and I walked in comfortable silence through the woods, both of us perfectly content. There was something so freeing, so renewing about being out in nature.

"Man, I wish we could do this every day," Tyler sighed.

"Me, too. I never feel more at peace than when I'm walking through the forest," I agreed. "Ever since I was a child, I knew I could always count on Mother Nature to get me feeling good again. No matter how much stress I was under, being out here and breathing the free, clean air helped me remember that all those little things that seemed so daunting back then were minuscule compared to the big picture. I guess for some people that would be frightening rather than comforting, but for me... well, I guess it's just nice to know I'm a part of something much larger than me, something I can never fully comprehend."

"That's beautiful, Mason," Tyler said softly. "I love the way you think."

I paused for a moment, so taken aback by the unusual compliment.

"You know, I don't think anyone's ever said anything like that to me. Thank you," I told him emphatically. Tyler just reached for my hand. We didn't need words. We could just be.

When we got back to the house, we were both feeling pretty worn out and in desperate need of a shower. While the waterfall and pool had certainly been refreshing, we were both craving some soap and lather before starting on our evening plans.

"You want to take turns? I'll let you go first," I offered to Tyler as I tugged off my hiking boots and set them in the closet.

He was already stripping off his damp clothes and dropping them into the hamper. My breath caught in my throat when I glanced over to see his taut, perfectly rounded bare ass. My cock stirred immediately, and I regretted suggesting we shower separately. But luckily enough, Tyler seemed to be on the same page. He turned around and gave me a sly smile.

"Why don't we just hop in there together?" he suggested innocently.

"You don't have to ask me twice," I enthused.

"Meet me in there, then," Tyler replied, heading down the hall to the bathroom.

I watched him walk away, my eyes riveted to his flawless butt. I hurriedly pulled off the rest of my clothes and rushed after him, throwing my arms around him just as he was about to turn on the shower. He chuckled and spun around to kiss me softly at first, then with more passion. He reached behind himself to turn on the shower, never even breaking our kiss. As the bathroom slowly filled with cozy, comforting hot steam, we stepped into the shower together. I sighed with pleasure as the warm water hit my body, and I moaned, pressing myself against the full length of Tyler's body. My arms fell around him, my hands stroking the hair back from his face as we kissed languidly.

"So," I murmured, "how did you like your surprise today?"

"It was amazing. Gorgeous," he whispered as he kissed along my jaw up to my ear. "You were the most stunning part of the view, though."

I chuckled, feeling a pleasurable shiver down my spine as he breathed hot, soft air against the shell of my ear. We leaned against one another, making a slow show of lathering each other up, breathing in the steam and fragrant, floral soapy scents as we washed one another's bodies, then our hair. All along, we murmured sweet nothings to each other, taking our time and enjoying every second of our shared shower experience. I kissed him deeply, letting my hands rove down his body. I delicately wrapped my fingers around his stiffening cock, and he sighed with approval, melting into my touch. I was pleasantly surprised when he slid his hand down to wrap around my hard shaft, the two of us sliding back and forth, up and down, in slick tandem. We both groaned, rocking against one another as the hot water beaded down our backs. We faced each other, kissing softly, swallowing back each other's sighs and moans as we gradually increased the pace. Tyler's hand slid expertly along the length of my cock, his thumb coming up to circle the sensitive head, making me shudder and gasp with need. We took our time, savoring the moment as we worked each other to the edge, then back down, over and over until we were both desperate for release. At the same time, we came all over each other, his spunk sliding down my stomach and vice versa. We swayed together under the hot water, rinsing off thoroughly as we came down from our shared high.

Finally, once we were totally clean and pruny-fingered, we got out and dried off. We dressed in comfy lounge clothes and headed into the kitchen together to start on a healthy, tasty dinner. I had a fire crackling in the fireplace and the soft strains of a jazz album playing from across the house. Tyler and I worked together so seamlessly—in the kitchen, in the shower, in the forest—everywhere. Being with him was so simple, so instinctual. It felt right, like we had been living this way all our lives. It was hard for me to envision now what my life had been like before he moved in, as though all those memories paled in comparison to the memories we were making together now. We kissed and lingered over the food prep, moving at our own pace and chatting softly about everything and nothing at the same time. We sat down to eat our feast of roast lemon chicken and quinoa salad, but we were interrupted when I got a phone call.

Still feeling lazy and content, I answered it with a yawning, "Hello?"

"Hey man. It's Hunter," came the voice on the other end.

"Oh. Hey. I'm here with Tyler—do you mind if I put you on speakerphone?" I said.

"Nah, go for it. Hi, Tyler!" he exclaimed.

I set the phone down on the table as Tyler and I started eating.

"What's up, Hunter?" I prompted.

"Listen, the big game is coming up before you know it, and I was hopin' to get the boys together on the field in a couple days so we can

124

run some plays and, you know, just get back into the swing of things. You two down?" he asked.

I glanced over at Tyler questioningly. He looked nervous for a moment, then a resigned expression crossed his face, and he nodded. "Yeah. We'll be there," he said confidently.

TYLER

"What do you think of what you see?" Mason asked from behind, and I jolted back to reality with a start, looking embarrassed as I rounded to face him.

It had been just a couple of days since we had gone for a hike in the woods, but this morning had been the first time I had really looked at myself in the mirror for a while. I had been entirely caught up between training for the game and letting things go wild at seemingly every turn with Mason, and I hadn't even thought to check on my progress.

Since today was the day we were heading to practice with the other guys we'd be playing alongside, it had hit me first thing in the morning that I ought to check it out. In all honesty, my heart had been pounding when I went into the bathroom to look at myself in the mirror, but now that I had seen it... the results spoke for themselves.

I turned my body to face Mason and ran my hand down my front. After two weeks, where there had once been a bit more flab than I was happy with, I felt smooth skin that hugged the tight muscle underneath. Some of that had been there the whole time, but now it was more pronounced than ever. I might not have the ridiculously tight six-pack that Mason had, but my stomach was flat and far tauter than it had been in years. That much was undeniable. I even saw the beginnings of a vee pointing down below my waistline, and I couldn't hold back a chuckle at that.

Mason ran his hands down the now trim muscles of my shoulders and biceps.

"I can't believe I didn't notice before now," I admitted, shaking my head at my own body in disbelief.

I brought my hands to my waist, and my eyes widened before I turned my body just enough to see my backside. The weight I had a month ago liked to build up around my hips and butt. Now though, I was stunned to see what was close to the same bubble butt I rocked back in high school. It wasn't exactly the same, of course, but I liked the new version better than the old, even.

"I've been noticing from start to finish," Mason said casually, sliding his hands down to my cock and fondling it. "And if you ask *me*, I'm a big fan of all twenty versions of your body I've seen so far. And I can say with confidence I'd be just as happy with you bigger than you started or trimmer than you are now," he added with a wink to the mirror.

"Well, be that as it may," I teased, rolling my eyes with a smile, exaggerating my accent while using a phrase you didn't hear much around Winchester, "I bet I'm a little more flexible in bed, not just out on the field."

"Don't talk like that if you have any hopes of us getting to practice today," Mason teased right back.

He pressed his hips against my backside, and I felt his mast between my cheeks, resting peacefully yet ominously. By now, I knew damn well to take that warning seriously. Mason wouldn't hesitate to make me his in a heartbeat...and I was never all that interested in stopping him. After all, we were making up for fifteen years of missed opportunity. And that was a lot of catching up to do.

"Seriously though," Mason said, turning me around to rest his shoulders on me and look at me with less flirty resolution. "Feeling good about today? This might not be the game, but it'll be the first time that we're really out there with our teammates."

"With you, I'd take on a real-ass pro football team." I laughed, and I reached around to clap my hand to his and exchange a firm squeeze.

"Then let's head out," Mason said, patting me on the ass and turning to walk back into the bedroom. "Wouldn't want to leave 'em hanging, would we?"

* * *

MY CAR PULLED up in the parking lot of the football field, where a number of cars were already parked. Most of the guys were already on the field, and Mason and I were greeted with shouts and waves as we got out of the car.

As soon as we approached, I saw Hunter break away from the group and come to join us, taking off his cap and giving a sloppy smile. I could tell he was in his element. As the high school coach, that was no surprise. He was getting to do what he'd always wanted to.

"Glad to see you two could make it," he said, falling in with us as we walked to the field. "We're just about to get started."

"Wouldn't miss it for the world," Mason said cheerfully, grinning at Hunter. "Speaking of, I had a few questions about the game, now that it's getting closer to the big day."

"You and everyone else." Hunter chuckled. "Come on, I'll start getting everyone together. I was just about to text you to make sure you'd make it, and the last guy we're waiting on is Marshall."

"And he moves when he's good and ready," I said with a laugh.

A few minutes later, we were all gathered on the bench... or at least, as many as could fit were sitting on the bench. We'd all grown a bit since high school, and I was surprised and a little relieved to see that I wasn't the only one who had put on some extra weight. I was sitting on the far end of the right side, and Mason stood beside me, arms crossed. As predicted, Marshall was the last guy to arrive. I had gotten so used to seeing Mason's figure that it was surprising to see someone just as tall and broad-shouldered crossing the field. It wasn't until Marshall stood next to Mason and gave everyone a curt, wordless nod that I realized he and Mason were about the same size and build.

"Glad we could all make it," Hunter finally said, grinning at all of us.

"Is this everyone-everyone?" I asked, looking around.

"Good question. Yes and no," Hunter explained. "You're all looking around at your teammates. Nothing about this game is official, obviously, and for the most part, we all know who is who's people. Since Bill and I are the ones organizing this match, we got together and sorted out teams as balanced as we could. We split the actual football players right down the middle, to keep things fair. Not everyone on the team could make it back for one reason or another, so anyone else who was interested in the game got distributed evenly between the teams. Sound good to y'all?"

We all gave a collective sound of agreement, and Hunter smiled.

"What about uniforms?" Mason asked. "I know a few of us might not have our old ones anymore."

"Glad someone asked that, too," Hunter said with a broad grin. "I made a few friends when I went off to college, and a few of them stayed in college football in one way or another. One of my buds got me a hookup for some spare sets of gear that I brought. I've got 'em in the back of my truck, so anyone who needs one can try them out."

"You can *say* it's 'cause some of us have beer guts now," said a guy from the far end of the bench, and we laughed good-naturedly while Mason grinned down at me proudly.

"All right, here's what I want to do here," Hunter said, clapping his hands. "We're not on a team, and this game ain't taking us to state. This here's a friendly match," he said with a wink. "Meaning, this is another shot at tackling the asshole you never settled your beef with back in the day."

A ripple of laughter went through our group, but Hunter waved us off.

"Kidding, kidding. Mostly. But Mason, Marshall, for the sake of you two, I *am* completely kidding. I don't want to see ambulance lights in the parking lot by the end of that game."

Mason nodded, and Marshall just gave an ominous chuckle.

"And speaking of," Hunter went on, "that brings me back to why I dragged your asses out of bed to be here this afternoon. I'm going to run us through some drills. We ain't old men yet, but some of us haven't used certain joints in a while, so I want to make sure nobody's going to have to explain to some doctor why he's in the emergency room over a high school reunion. So we'll start things slow and ramp up the scale until it's dark. Sound good?"

"Hell yeah," I said, and the rest of the group joined in a collective and resounding *yes*.

We started out with some light jogging to warm us up. The second we all took off around the football field, I felt energized in a way I hadn't in a long time. With each step I took, the feeling of the earth under my feet just felt plain *right*. It was a warmer afternoon than the day Mason and I had gone out, signaling that, as predicted, we were in the death throes of spring, and it would be early summer weather just as the game started.

Jogging with Mason had become such a second nature to me by now that I barely even thought about it. The two of us were off together in perfect harmony, and with Mason at my side, each breath of the rich country air I drew in felt that much more invigorating. But after just a few minutes of jogging, I realized that it felt a little quieter than I had expected. I glanced over my shoulder, then snapped my attention back to the front with wide eyes.

Mason and I weren't just keeping up; we were leading the pack. Marshall was hot on our tails, practically keeping pace with us, and Carter was right there with him, but most of the rest of the team was lagging just far enough behind that it was a noticeable difference.

I cast a sidelong glance at Mason, and I saw that he was smiling too, probably at my reaction. He confirmed this when he looked over long enough to wink.

"Nice to see a payoff, huh?" he said quietly.

"Let's not get cocky." I chuckled, even though I absolutely agreed. "We've got a long day ahead of us."

That did not begin to describe the day we were going to have.

Hunter was a pretty laid-back guy, but it turned out that when he was playing coach, he could run a tight shift. The next drill he ran us through was meant to test our agility a little more directly. He had us crab-running from side to side on the field in rows of five each, and with the sharp cry of a whistle, he'd have us reverse direction and head the other way. This time, I realized that the game wouldn't just be a cakewalk despite the training Mason and I had put in. Slimming down was one thing, but playing football was another.

Still, I managed to hold my own better than I'd thought I would. My body served me in ways it hadn't since high school, and I remembered the way certain movements felt bit by bit. I had to admit it was thrilling once my heart really got pumping and my muscles were warmed up.

And that wasn't all Hunter had on the menu for dexterity training. He ran us through tires, forcing us to jump and show off how nimble we could be under pressure by hopping leg to leg from tire to tire in a sequence. We weren't just measuring individual strength. We had to be a strong, functioning team.

Mason, of course, had no problems doing any of this. I could barely tell that he wasn't a high school football player. He moved so effortlessly that I almost suspected he had been doing some secret training off-hours, but then I remembered that it was quite literally his job to be able to do all this. Marshall and Carter once again shone as the other powerhouses of the drills, and I was beginning to see that we had our MVPs in those three.

Things got a little more intense from there. Hunter wanted to see how strong we were, so next was time for resistance training. There were groans from some of the team as Hunter wheeled out the dreaded training dummies.

These things were essentially big punching bags about the size and shape of a football player, and they were affixed by metal bars to a metal grill that lay flat against the ground, while the dummies leaned forward. The idea behind the drill was to manually push those dummies across the field. It was resistance training that taught you how to push immense weight like that and simulate the feeling of bodies crashing on the field.

And like the other drills, this wasn't about individualism. Each piece of equipment had four dummies on it, which meant that everyone had to be pushing at the same time, at the same pace, or you'd either go spinning or go too slow. None of us had touched these dummies since high school, so there was a general murmur of grateful approval when Mason was the first man to step forward and volunteer to try them out.

I joined him next, and right behind me came Marshall and Carter. We took our places on a line, posed to take off. Hunter stood at the ready, lips on his whistle, and with a sharp blow, he brought his hand down, and we took off.

My vision focused on the dummy, and as I charged it, I felt the rush in my veins in those vital moments that I put one leg in front of the other, barreling forward with all my weight. Just then, I wasn't just Tyler. I felt like the player I'd been just fifteen years ago, and I was out for battle.

Our bodies crashed into the dummies almost at the same time. I could have sworn Mason and Marshalls' dummies nearly bent backward at the immense strength that met them, while Carter and I took up the ends. I had to turn my face to grip the dummy properly, and as I dug my feet into the turf and pushed forward, I saw Mason. His body worked like a fine-tuned machine. His brow was knit, and sweat glistened on his forehead as his rippling muscles flexed. I watched his calf muscles turning, driving the dummy forward, and his tight tank top hugged his back and showed off every ridge that gave Mason his strength.

But even as I watched him, I realized that my body was working in much the same way. My mind had been dazed for a moment on impact, but that passed quickly, and my legs were moving with almost as much power as Mason's. In unison, we drove the dummy stand forward, and we heard the cheers of the other guys at our backs with every step. It felt like we had only been pushing for a few seconds, but one by one, we realized we were pushing past the halfway line, and we came to a stop.

Our faces were red, even Marshall's, but all of us looked around at each other with big, sloppy grins on our faces. The guys on the bench were applauding enthusiastically. After high-fiving Mason and Marshall, my palm hurt worse than any other part of my body, and Carter's didn't do much to help, but I didn't care. I was laughing, and my heart was thumping hard in a good way.

I might have started training to lose weight, but being out here with the guys, I knew that win or lose, I was eager to hit the field again. With Mason at my back, I was going to take this game head on.

MASON

I WAS POSITIVELY THRUMMING WITH EXCITEMENT AS I CLOCKED OUT OF my shift at five o'clock on Tuesday evening. I walked over to the front desk to sit and wait for Tyler to come pick me up, my whole body buzzing. Apparently my enthusiasm was visible because Liz came strolling up to me with her eyes narrowed, a look of amusement and suspicion on her face. She sat in the swivel chair next to me with her arms folded over her chest, sizing me up.

"What? What are you looking at? You're making me nervous," I said with a laugh.

"You! I'm looking at you," she said. "You seem... different somehow."

"Really? What do you mean?" I asked, fully aware of what she meant.

"You just look really happy about something. Oh my god. Are you quitting?" she gasped.

I burst out laughing and shook my head. "God, no! I love my job. Why would I quit working here, Liz?" I chuckled.

"Well, you look like you're glowing, but unless you've got different plumbing than I thought, I don't think you could possibly be pregnant. I'm trying to figure out what else it could be," she joked good-naturedly.

"Can't a guy just be happy for no reason these days?" I mused.

"No," she said matter-of-factly. "In this world? No. Definitely not. There's something going on here, and I want to get to the bottom of it."

"Don't you have a bunch of people to torture somewhere?" I asked.

"Nah. Last Zumba class of the day was at three. I'm a free agent now," she said, waggling her eyebrows suggestively.

I snorted. "Maybe we should be giving you more work to do, then," I warned.

She rolled her eyes, knowing that I was teasing. Technically, I *was* her boss since I had seniority over most of the employees here at the gym, but I much preferred to keep my team feeling all equal to one another. I figured it was better for morale and camaraderie that way. Besides, I found it kind of distasteful to have to boss people around like some frowning overseer. I liked teamwork, not delegation.

"Don't change the subject. I want to know what it is you've got goin' on that's making you so happy," Liz pressed. "Oh! Oh my god. Are you engaged?"

I groaned. "Good lord, woman. No. Tyler and I are just casual."

"Casual? Living together and spending every free moment together is casual now?" she prompted with a giggle. "Because if so, I might have to break the news to Kate that she and I aren't as serious as we thought we were."

"It's different, all right? You and Kate... you're official," I said.

"Ah, and you and Tyler aren't? Have you had The Talk yet?" she asked, now more helpful than nosy.

She leaned in with genuine interest, wanting to help. This was part of why I adored her so much as a friend and coworker. Once you pushed past her fortress of sarcasm and dry wit, she was actually a very dedicated, attentive listener. Even though she was considerably younger than I was, Liz was fairly wise for her years. Kate, on the other hand, was interminably cheerful and sweet, but too naive to be of much help in deep discussions. The two of them made a very even-keeled, well-rounded pair, which I found to actually be a boon to our work environment rather than a hindrance.

"Well, not really," I admitted, but before I could say anything else, my phone lit up and interrupted our conversation.

I grinned and jumped to my feet when I read the text, which was Tyler letting me know he had just pulled up outside the gym to collect me.

"That him?" Liz said.

I nodded, grabbing my gym bag and slinging it over my shoulder. "Yep. See you tomorrow, Liz," I replied.

"See ya. Tell Ty I said hi," she chimed after me.

"Will do!" I called back as I hurried out to Tyler's car.

It was drizzling ever so slightly, and I sheltered my head with my bag as I slid into the passenger seat. Tyler was beaming at me warmly, as he always did when he picked me up, although I thought I detected a sort of glimmer to his eyes that was new.

"Hey man. How was work?" he asked as he drove the car out of the parking lot and out onto the main road through Winchester.

"Good. Good. I thought we were going to work out a little bit tonight, though?" I asked.

"Sorry for the change of plans. I just couldn't wait to show you my surprise for you," he admitted with a big grin. "I can't wait to see the look on your face."

I raised an eyebrow. "What is it? Should I be concerned?" I chuckled.

"No. Actually, you're going to be over the moon. Trust me," he replied.

For a while I wasn't sure what to expect—maybe he had planned out a dinner date for us or an evening jog in some picturesque nature setting. But as we drove on, I began to realize that we were headed in the direction of the garage where Tyler worked. My heart began to pound like crazy as we pulled into the big lot out back of the garage.

"No way," I murmured breathlessly, shaking my head.

"Yes way," Tyler joked, nudging me on the shoulder.

"Are you serious? Is this really happening?" I asked.

Tyler laughed and gestured for me to follow him out of the car. "Yep. Sure is. Real as anything. Come on, let me show you," he said.

We climbed out of the Chevelle, and he led me to the garage, where my beautiful truck was sitting, pretty and pristine as the day she was manufactured. My jaw dropped, and I felt a rush of powerful emotions wash over me, riveting me to the spot. I could hardly believe my eyes. Not only had Tyler managed to fix the massive technical issues going on with her, but he had waxed and glossed her until she was shining brightly. I even felt a momentary prickle of happy tears burning in my eyes, but I hastily blinked them back before rushing over to throw my arms around Tyler.

"Holy cow. Thank you. I can't even... I can't believe this is happening. You're a damn genius, Ty!" I raved, hugging him tight.

He patted me on the back softly, laughing under his breath. "You're welcome. It turned out to be fairly simple once I ran the diagnostics. Took a lot of labor and precision, but she should be back on the road and running like new now," he explained proudly.

I pushed back and gazed into his face, shaking my head with pure awe.

"You are unreal, you know that?" I murmured.

Tyler's cheeks flushed pink, and it took all my strength not to kiss him right then and there, but I had something else in mind.

"We should celebrate!" I burst out. "I can't wait to drive her."

"I can think of the perfect place to go for her maiden voyage," Tyler said.

"The Chisel?" I guessed.

"The Chisel," he agreed with a big grin.

He gave me back my keys, and I hopped into the truck, running my hands over the smooth leather interior, breathing in the familiar car smell that flooded my nostrils as I closed myself in. I started up the engine, holding my breath, and was elated to hear it purr smoothly. Tyler got into his car, and the two of us drove out of the lot, heading across town to The Chisel, which was located just within the city limits.

All the while, I was smiling like a maniac, overjoyed to have my beloved truck back in fighting condition. None of the usual bumps and shakes were present now, and she drove like a dream. I couldn't wrap my head around the amount of hard, cautious, deliberate work Tyler must have poured into getting her back on the road, especially when I thought back to what Chett, the other mechanic, had said about the issues being insurmountable. Tyler had literally done the impossible. He had given me back my freedom, my happiness, my pride and joy. I realized in that moment that regardless of what happened in that football game coming up, no matter what direction Tyler and I ended up going on the journey of our relationship (if that was what I might call it), I would be eternally grateful to him for this wonderful gift. No one had ever given me something this great, this valuable. My heart swelled with warmth and affection for Tyler. I couldn't wait to get to the bar and buy him as many drinks as he so desired. He deserved it. He deserved the world.

We pulled up to the bar and parked our vehicles side by side, then hopped out and hooked our arms together. "How'd she feel on the road?" Tyler asked me as we headed to the back entrance of The Chisel.

"She drove like a damn dream, Tyler. You really outdid yourself. I'm in awe," I admitted.

He blushed again, looking both pleased and bashful at once. God, he was adorable.

"That's wonderful to hear. It took a lot of hours, but it was so worth it. I actually learned a lot about vintage trucks in the process," he remarked.

I pushed open the door to The Chisel, and we were instantly greeted by a tall, broad-shouldered guy wearing a faint scowl on his roguishly handsome face. He gave us a once-over, then smiled and nodded us through once he realized who we were.

"What's up, Marshall?" I greeted him with a fist bump.

"Nothin' much. Just a rowdy crew in here tonight," he replied gruffly.

He was a regular here who often doubled as a doorman because of his intimidating height and muscles. Funnily enough, though, I sensed there was a really nice guy underneath all that rough-and-tumble demeanor.

"Nice to see you again," Tyler said, stretching out a hand for him to shake like the good Southern boy he was. "Are you excited about the match comin' up soon?"

"Hell yeah, man. Looking forward to the opportunity to absolutely cream some of those guys on the field. I've got a lot of stress to take out on an appropriate target, if you know what I mean. Who better to take it than our opponents, eh?" he joked.

"Glad to have you on our side, that's for sure," I remarked.

He gave me a wink. "The feeling is mutual, man. Have a great night. I might join you for a drink in a bit if you don't mind a third wheel," he said.

"Of course not. Join us whenever," Tyler said brightly.

We walked up to the crowded bar, managing somehow to find ourselves a pair of open stools to perch on. I pretty quickly managed to catch the eye of Parker, the bartender on shift tonight. He slid down in front of us with a bit of a harried smile.

"Busy crowd tonight, huh?" I said.

He nodded, rolling his eyes. "Yeah. It's a Tuesday, but you'd think it was Friday judging by the atmosphere. What can I do for you boys this evening?" he asked.

"Two beers. Whatever you've got on tap. You know what I like," I replied.

"Sure thing, man," Parker said and hurried off to get our beers.

"You still ridin' the high from driving your truck again?" Tyler murmured, leaning in.

I nodded. "Hell yeah. I have a feeling I'm going to be on cloud nine for a while. If you need me, you know where to find me. Just look up," I joked.

"I'm real glad to hear that. Seeing you so happy makes me happy," Tyler commented.

"Same to you, Ty. You're really making a difference in your fitness and health lately. You look better than ever," I told him truthfully.

He looked away, a smile playing on his lips as the blush crept across his cheeks. "It's all thanks to you, you know. Without your help, I would never have made this kind of progress. And it feels so good. It's not even the pounds I've lost, really. It's just that I feel better overall. Like my body is capable of much more than it used to be," he explained.

"Perfect. That's exactly the right way to think about it. After all, the weight isn't what matters most at the end of the day. I just want you to feel good in your own skin, Tyler. You deserve that," I said.

"Thank you. I'm really glad we've been able to work together. Not over yet, though," he added with a wink.

"No, not yet," I agreed.

I smiled, even as my heart sank. I remembered suddenly that there was meant to be an endpoint to our arrangement, and it was swiftly approaching. Now that my truck was fixed up, that meant Tyler's end of the bargain had been fulfilled. What was left now was the football match, and that was coming up fast. I had come to really treasure the time I got to spend with Tyler, and the thought of it all coming to an end made my heart ache like nothing else. I could tell, as we both sipped our beers and danced around the subject, that Tyler was trying to avoid talking about it as much as I was. In a way that was reassuring. It gave me hope that maybe Tyler was starting to feel the same way I was, that this was turning into more than just the quid quo pro we had originally settled on. I had real feelings for Tyler. Strong ones. And they weren't going anywhere anytime soon. Maybe ever. But what was going to become of us once that game came and passed? How would we make things work once we jumped the biggest hurdle together? Would we return to our respective separate lives and leave our emotions behind? Or would we find a way to make it work and continue... as a real couple?

Every cell in my body was desperately hoping for the latter scenario, but I couldn't know for sure that Tyler wanted the same thing. I was just about to work up the courage to ask him outright when we were crudely interrupted by a pair of big, burly guys stumbling into us at the counter. They drunkenly knocked into Tyler hard enough to spill his beer all over the counter, and when they realized their mistake, they didn't apologize. They only guffawed like hyenas.

And when I recognized who they were, it didn't surprise me. The guys were two who played on the team with us. They were slated to be on the opposing team for the 'friendly' match: Jared and Bill.

"Oh, my bad. Didn't see you there," Bill slurred.

"No problem, man," Tyler said softly.

"Hey, look who it is!" shouted Jared over the din of the crowd and the jukebox.

Tyler tried to shy away, but Jared rudely grabbed him by the shoulder to jerk him back, making me see red. I gritted my teeth and got to my feet, preparing to step in and fight if I needed to. I hadn't kept up with Bill and Jared post-graduation, mostly because they were a couple of assholes, even back then. We had been civil enough with each other to play as a team in high school, but nowadays? I had no obligation to put up with their bullshit.

"You two the ones drivin' those junkers outside?" Bill snorted.

Again, rage bubbled up inside my chest. I bit my tongue as Tyler calmly replied, "The Chevelle and truck? Yes. Those belong to us. They're vintage."

"They're vintage?" Jared cackled. "What are you, ninety-year-old women?"

"Careful, man. Back off," I warned in a low growl.

Jared held up both hands in mock surrender, still grinning like a fool.

"Don't worry. We're not here to start a fight. We're savin' up all our energy for the football game," Bill piped up, his eyes glassy.

"Great. We're looking forward to a little competition," I said.

"Hopefully we can all remember how to cooperate," Tyler said icily.

"And look at you!" Jared blurted out, jabbing a finger in Tyler's face. "Must be spendin' lots of time on the treadmill, eh? Lookin' good, man. But let me make one thing very clear: losin' a couple pounds won't make you eighteen again."

Bill burst out laughing at the mean joke, and I hastily led Tyler away from them to a quiet corner table where we could hopefully sip the rest of our beer in peace. Tyler looked pale and shaken up by their cruel words, which made me want to kick their asses, but I knew I needed to hold it together. If things got too out of hand, Marshall was around to keep it under control. I was better off tending to Tyler's wounded pride than starting a bar brawl.

"Don't listen to them," I said quietly. "They're drunk. And stupid."

"Yeah, I know," Tyler sighed. "But… they have a point, right?"

"No. No, they do not," I said firmly, shaking my head. "You've worked your ass off to get where you are now. Don't let them get into your head. They're just messing with you because we've got that game coming up. Keep your eyes on the prize. Besides, we're here to celebrate tonight. You brought my truck back to life when I thought nobody could. That is amazing. You are amazing, Tyler. I need you to know that."

He smiled faintly, then sipped his beer. "Thank you. I appreciate it," he said softly.

"And you know what? We're gonna kick their asses all up and down that field, you hear me? We're going to win," I proclaimed.

A couple of our fellow team members joined us at the corner table, and we spent the next hour or so talking strategy and bonding. Eventually Marshall ended up kicking Jared and Bill out of the bar before coming over to join our conversation. The night took a turn for the better, and before long, we were all joking and laughing again. At the end of the evening, with a few pints in our bellies, Tyler and I made the decision that we would continue living and working out together at least until the big game. For now, I swallowed back down my wish that it could continue after that. I could only hope.

TYLER

DESPITE THE CONFIDENCE I HAD BEEN ABLE TO WHIP UP LAST NIGHT, BY the next day, I wasn't feeling quite as good about what we were going up against soon. It was late afternoon, and I was driving home from work, taking the long way. "Taking the long way" was my euphemism for having forgotten that I don't have to pick Mason up anymore, and I had driven almost all the way to the gym before remembering that. The day around me was coming to a peaceful close, and the sun was out for longer than either of us had seen all season. I always could have sworn the land itself enjoyed the daylight as much as the people did. The sunsets always seemed more restful and less weary during the spring and summer. Maybe that was just me, though.

I drove with the windows down, and I enjoyed the warm air whipping around my face and over my skin as I let one elbow hang out the window. I just enjoyed the feeling of the outdoors rushing through the car. Hell, I even liked seeing dust get kicked up and whipped out into the breeze. It felt clean.

Maybe I was getting ahead of myself with this game. It had felt like a rush to be out there training again, but training and playing were two very different things, and I was letting those stupid assholes' words get to me. That was the long and short of it, as much as I wanted to beat around the bush and tell myself there were a dozen other little things to worry about.

I hated to admit it, but it was true that fifteen years couldn't exactly make me a high school athlete, could it? I had no doubts about the way I felt about the changes I had made. Even if Mason weren't reminding me every time he got the chance, I only had to look in the mirror to remind myself why I started doing this in the first place.

I felt good and healthy, something I hadn't felt in a long time. But now, when I looked in the mirror, I saw bright eyes and clear skin that looked healthier than ever. I'd even say my hair looked better, fuller. I had more energy throughout the day, which kept me happier and more productive.

Frankly, I felt like a new man, and I don't know that I could have done it without Mason's help. And that was the thing: could I keep up with Mason? Would I be able to deliver when he stormed the gridiron?

Mason was incredible. He didn't just have a perfect body, but his mind was a machine, too. He was lined up to give a class presentation soon at college, and he had been nervous about that, but the fact that he was there doing that at all was impressive to me.

My body warmed at the thought of how I had comforted him this morning when he was expressing anxiety about that presentation. I might not have been much help studying, but if there was one thing I could do, it was make that mind and body feel all the more relaxed and relieved before a big show like a presentation.

I rested my head back against the seat and gripped the steering wheel tighter, clenching my jaw. Back when I was younger, I tended to get away from everything whenever life got too overwhelming. A thoughtful smile crossed my lips as I wondered if that was something else I was too old for.

There was one way to find out.

When I turned onto the last road leading toward Mason's house, I noticed his truck turning onto it from the opposite direction. I grinned and gave him a wave, and we pulled into the driveway one after the other.

"If I didn't know better, I'd say you were following me," Mason said as he climbed out of his truck and met me halfway across the driveway. We clapped our hands together and pulled each other into a hug.

"Maybe I was. You have a nice house," I teased, and I gave him a quick peck on the cheek.

"Is everything okay?" he asked, reaching up and rubbing my neck with one of his big hands as we headed inside. "You looked a little down before you noticed me. Or was I just seeing things?"

It was remarkable how perceptive Mason could be, considering he was the type of guy who theoretically only worked with the human body. But then again, maybe that was what helped him pick up on nonverbal cues easier than other people. He knew the human body better than most.

"Yeah, yeah, I'm good," I lied, chuckling and trying to ignore the distinct I-don't-believe-you look Mason was giving me. "But hey, I was thinking, did you want to go on a quick hike before dinner tonight? I had a trail in mind that's pretty short, figured we could toss the ball back and forth a little."

Mason gave me a searching look, trying to figure out what I was really getting at. But that soon melted away because an afternoon hike was something Mason rarely turned down.

"Sure thing," he said, holding up his bag of gym clothes. "Let's get changed and head out so we can beat the sunset."

About fifteen minutes later, I pulled up to a small, empty parking lot with a couple of picnic benches adjacent to them, and a single unmarked trail leading away from the area. The place barely looked like it had changed a day.

"Less of a hiking trail, more of a walk through the park?" Mason asked, winking at me as he got the football out of the back seat. "You could have just asked me out on a date, you know."

"I could have, but it's more fun with the surprise." I chuckled. "But really, this isn't anything huge, so don't get too amped up."

"Not getting amped up is a pretty tall order when I'm running through the woods with you," he fired back with a smug smile.

When he wanted to, Mason knew just how to get me smiling and so flustered that I let my guard down. The next moment, the leather ball came flying my direction, and without a second thought, I caught it and cradled it to my chest with practiced ease. Mason jogged on ahead of me, and I tossed the ball back to him. He jumped and caught it at the entrance to the trail, and I couldn't keep the grin off my face as I hurried after him.

We started off on the trail just like that, tossing the ball back and forth to each other to the sound of the afternoon buzz of insects, birds, and squirrels all around us. One squirrel seemed to find our presence offensive enough that it bark-chirped at us from the trees for what felt like half a mile before it lost interest and scurried off.

"So, what made you think of this old place?" Mason asked once we'd gone far enough into the woods that I could see our destination. "I haven't been here since...god, back in school, it must have been."

"Yeah, actually, same," I said as I caught the ball.

I pointed in the direction of a cluster of gnarled old trees near a rock formation a little ways off the path. Mason took my cue and jogged in that direction, watching the ground to keep an eye out for holes, and he caught the ball I tossed him with ease. Throwing through the woods was a bit of a challenge, but that made it interesting. Mason tossed the ball back to me, and as I did a running jump to catch it, I jogged after him over to the rock formation, gesturing broadly to it.

"I just wanted to come out here and make sure the old hideout of mine was still standing," I explained, looking fondly up at the humble little landmark. "Place looked a lot bigger back in the day. That shouldn't be a surprise though, yeah?" I chuckled.

"Hideout?" Mason asked, coming to stand by my side. "What, like a place you'd come to crash sometimes? I thought you said things were pretty good for you when you were a kid."

"Oh, no, nothing like that." I chuckled, and I trudged closer to it, walking around its diameter a few paces until I came to what I was looking for.

It was a nook in the woods, between a pair of mighty old beech trees that had formed what I thought was a perfect little seat for getting cozy.

"It doesn't look like much, but this is where I used to come to read whenever I needed to get away from everything," I said, giving Mason a sheepish smile as I gestured to my nook. "I think I found it one day when I was... I dunno, pretty young. I just remember getting into some mystery book for kids, plopping down, and tearing through the thing until it was too dark out to read."

"Wow," Mason said, putting his hands on his hips and grinning around at the thought. "I've gotta say, I wasn't much of a reader back then, but if I'd found this place, I would have been tempted."

"Right?" I said, feeling elated that Mason was impressed by what I thought was a little slice of paradise. "I dunno, it's just cozy. And between the trees and the rock, most of the noise from around the woods gets canceled out. Not that it's ever wild out here."

I stepped into the nook and cleared some of the leaves on the ground so that I could take a seat, and I couldn't keep the smile off my face at the feeling of the familiar spot under me. Mason leaned against one of the trees and put his leg up on the other as he folded his arms, sort of trapping me in the nook while I reclined.

"So this was where you came for you-time, huh?" he asked. "Pretty idyllic if you ask me. I'm jealous."

"I came here when I needed to shut everything out," I said. "Sometimes, between school and the team, I just felt overwhelmed. I could find some quiet time at home, sure, but that wasn't the same as being *alone*. You know what I mean?"

"God, do I ever." Mason chuckled as I tossed him the ball. "The gym was that for me, honestly. Even though it was crowded, it was a place I could go, and nobody would bother me if I put my headphones in and just got lost in the workout."

"You were already in pretty perfect shape back then," I pointed out. "No wonder you landed the job you did."

"I would have been in hot water if I hadn't gotten it," Mason admitted, grinning down at me, but I raised a confused eyebrow.

"Didn't you get offered the job right out of high school?" I asked.

"Yes and no," Mason said, and his grin settled into a remarkably peaceful smile. "I… don't go spreading this around, but I could have gone to college easy if I'd wanted to."

"Well, sure you could've," I said. "Whether you like it or not, Mason, you're a guy who gets places."

"My case was a little specific. I… had a football scholarship waiting on me," he explained with a shadow of hesitation. "Could've been playing college football right out the doors. I don't know where that career would have taken me, but the doors were open."

"You're kidding," I breathed, raising my eyebrows. "I had heard the rumors, but…"

"But I'd made sure they didn't get around," Mason said, looking meaningfully at me.

"Why didn't you take the chance, man?" I asked, half laughing. "That would have been wild! See the country, live the life, fly across the gridiron as long as your body would let you. Didn't that sound good to you back then?"

"Maybe, but I can travel more than just the country outside that." I chuckled. "What, has Mark and Carter's trip to South America got you feeling adventurous?"

"Maybe a little," I admitted. "Don't get me wrong, I'd like to stay in Winchester as long as it's still standing, but a dream vacation down to the Caribbean has always sounded good."

"Yeah, somewhere warm and sandy with a piña colada and a little food to indulge in a vacation the right way," Mason said wistfully. "But do you remember that storm that hit the summer of our senior year? The one with the hurricane force gusts that damaged the school so badly they had to cancel summer classes?"

"Of course, yeah," I said.

Mason's mom was one of the many woodworkers around town, like my own mom was on a smaller scale. But while my mom worked out of her home, Mason's had a small shop of her own. Winchester's premier tourist attraction produced so many jobs that it was more remarkable if you met a couple who *neither* of them was a woodworker in some capacity.

"I don't know if you remember seeing my mom's studio when it was shut down, but it was the storm that did it," Mason said. "It did a number on the roof, and some debris from the neighboring businesses got blown through the windows of the place. You could barely recognize it when we pulled up to it."

"I had no idea," I admitted, running my hand through my hair. "There was a lot of car damage after that storm, so my dad had me working the garage harder than ever, especially since it was my first summer out of school."

"Turns out, that was a great excuse for me to stay home," Mason said. "My folks were all ready to send me off to college anyway, but I hung back to help repair houses over the summer and into the fall. For most of that year, my days were running back and forth between hitting the gym and doing repairs, doing any errands I could to take the pressure off."

"Shit, Mace," I said, "that's... a lot to do for your family. They must be proud of you. You're a hell of a good son," I added, elbowing his leg affectionately.

"All right now." He chuckled, reaching down and giving me a hand up, which I accepted. "I don't go spreading that story around, and I didn't tell you that just to give me some brownie points. Let's start walking back home. It's getting late."

"Doesn't make it less true," I teased, bumping my hip to his and smirking.

"Well, I figured that if you brought me somewhere you used to go to get away from everything, it meant something was bothering you," Mason said, tossing the ball from hand to hand as my face blushed red. "And I think I have a pretty good idea of what it is. You're thinking we should have done Marshall's job for him at The Chisel the other night and tossed those jerks out the window."

"Well..." I trailed off, scratching the back of my head.

"Hey, I'm right there with you," Mason said. "But the important part is not to let what they said get to you. Tyler, I'm a guy who could have been a college football QB, and I'm telling you I *want* you out there on the field with me. If you get out there, the only thing

149

you could possibly let down is Bill and Jared's hopes that you'll back out."

My face burned. It still amazed me how easily Mason could see through me, but then again, I never made much of an effort to hide my feelings. In my line of work, it just wasn't necessary.

"And if that isn't good enough..." Mason started before I could reply.

He put a hand on my shoulder and spun me around, then guided me backward to the nearest tree on the side of the road. Before I could react, he put his hands on my hips and his lips to mine, and he pushed his groin into me. I felt a quickly hardening shaft against my own, and I drew in a sharp breath.

Mason's hands worked their way around back to my ass, and he squeezed my cheeks and groaned into our kiss. When it finally broke, he glared at me, eyes mere inches apart.

"...then maybe a little old-fashioned stress relief is what you need," he growled. "Get the picture, Tyler? I want you, no matter where we are. We're going to kick ass together out there, and until then, I'm going to remind you every day of all the good things your body can do for both of us."

I tried to muster a response, but Mason's hand was going into my pants. He pushed the waist down far enough to expose my cock, and I felt the breeze cool it before Mason's warm hand wrapped around it. He started to massage the thick shaft, and it swelled larger with every pump.

"Fuck," I finally managed to breathe.

"Don't think that's a good enough answer," Mason teased, narrowing his eyes and bringing his mouth to my neck.

His thumb brushed against the bulging tip of my cock, and it pulsed as my heart raced. I hadn't been expecting this, in all honesty, but I wasn't about to try and stop him—not that I wanted to. I put a hand on Mason's powerful bicep and felt the muscles working in harmony to rub my cock, and my balls felt all their daily tension welling up at his touch. I wanted him so badly; I always did. He could do things to my body that nobody else could, things I never dreamed possible. Even something as simple as a hand job in the woods felt so much more powerful, more overwhelming than ever before.

"Are you gonna have my back out there like I know you can, Tyler?" he growled. "We're teammates. Always have been. I want to hear that you're going to meet me out there and give them hell. Not a single one of those assholes can hold a candle to you. Because you and I, we're unstoppable."

I used my other hand to clutch the back of the tree as I felt my orgasm getting closer and closer. I clenched my jaw as that relentless pace, that utter disregard for patience finally did me in. I sucked in a breath through my teeth as Mason's hand made me come, and he pressed a kiss to me as he kept my whole body pinned against the tree while I released.

Finally, the last of me was spent. Mason brought his hand up to his mouth without breaking eye contact, and a quick swipe of his tongue took care of a drop of white on his knuckle. He arched an eyebrow and looked at me as if expecting an answer.

"Yeah," I breathed, voice husky and exhausted. "Yeah, man. Let's give 'em hell."

MASON

I SAT IN THE BACK OF THE CLASSROOM, TAPPING MY FINGERTIPS ON THE desk nervously as I waited through the first few presentations. My classmates were going up one by one to give their exit presentations in front of the class, and with every presentation that went by, the closer and closer we got to the moment when I would have to give mine. I had never been a fan of public speaking. In fact, I had hated it so much that back in high school, when my parents had urged me to join a public speaking club as an extracurricular activity to pad out my resume, I had doggedly avoided it by trying out for the football team instead. It had seemed like kind of a long shot at the time. Sure, I had been a football fan since I was a young kid (kind of came with the territory of living in a small town in the South), and I had been muscular and built, even back then, but I had never before put much thought into the prospect of *playing* football.

That is, until I had stepped out onto that green turf for the first time and breathed in the grassy air, felt the fuzzy white lights on my skin, and lived the thrill of catching that pigskin and booking it down the field. From that very first moment at football tryouts, I had been hooked. I had gone into it assuming I wouldn't make the team, purely because everyone else seemed to know the game much more intimately than I did. But as it turned out, I was a natural at it. I had been picked for the varsity team, which had made my father tear up with happiness when I told him, and made my mom worry incessantly about head and bone injuries and an inflated ego. Lucky for her, I was an aggressive yet cautious player. I strategized in my head. I took measured risks. And I managed to come out the other side of it a stronger, more confident guy with a persisting love of exercise science. And wasn't that what had led me here to this moment today?

"...and that is why I plan to specialize in hydrotherapy," concluded one of my classmates, a vivacious girl named Becca. She smiled at the class, and we all responded with applause as she went to take her seat, looking utterly relieved to have the presentation over with.

"Very good. Thank you, Becca," said my professor, Dr. Stone.

She was a middle-aged woman with a shock of curly red hair and intense brown eyes, a former college sports medic who had come to Winchester to teach classes. I was eternally grateful for her decision to come here because it wasn't until she showed up that our local community college even offered this course. I only hoped my presentation and final grades would go as well as Becca's would. I didn't want to let my professor down, of course. Or myself. But tonight there was an extra level of nervousness placed on my shoulders because Tyler was here with me to watch my presentation. He was my ride to and from class anyway (my truck was fixed, but Tyler wanted to drive me one last time), so tonight he decided to just stay and hang around. I was simultaneously delighted and horrified. I loved having him here, of course, but I worried I might make a fool of myself. He seemed to sense my anxiety, as usual, and laid a calming hand softly on my arm, leaning close with a gentle smile.

"You'll be great. Don't worry," he whispered.

I forced what was probably an unconvincing smile. "Thanks. I hope so," I murmured.

"You nervous, too?" asked the classmate in front of me, a young guy named Todd.

I nodded. "Yeah. Little bit. I hate public speaking, to be honest," I said.

He winced. "Me too. The last time I had to give a big presentation like this was in high school, believe it or not. I've done everything to avoid it since then because it was... uh, not very pleasant. I ended up vomiting onstage in front of everybody," he admitted.

"Wow," Tyler and I said at the same time.

Todd sighed. "Yeah. Exactly."

"Well, I bet tonight you'll do just fine," I assured him. "But just in case, I'm going to stay here in the back row when you do your speech."

"Ha-ha," he said, rolling his eyes good-naturedly. "But seriously... that's a good idea. You know, just in case."

"Mason Glass," announced Dr. Stone. I froze up instantly, my eyes going wide.

Tyler nudged me gently. "Hey. That's you. Give 'em hell," he hissed.

My heart began to pound as I fumbled to get my papers into a neat stack. I rose slowly from my desk and walked to the front of the classroom, all eyes on me. I looked around at the sea of faces, most of them open and comforting, but still a lot to take in. I cleared my throat hoarsely and took a long, slow breath. It was crazy how I was a fully confident and self-assured adult, and yet standing in front of a class to give a presentation could still flood my veins with adrenaline and fear just like it used to do to me in high school. I guessed some things never change.

"Good evening, everybody. As you know by now, my name is Mason Glass, and I work at the local gym here in Winchester as a personal trainer. My intention in taking this course is to get certified in physical therapy so I can better serve my community. The nearest hospital is still a few towns over, but my gym has most of the necessary equipment for therapeutic training, so I hope to use what I've learned here to build a more convenient place for Winchesterites to heal a little bit closer to home," I began.

I swallowed back the lump in my throat, looking around the classroom. My eyes fell over every single face, including my professor's unreadable expression. I felt a little queasy until my gaze fell to Tyler, who was beaming at me with such genuine pride and adoration that I instantly relaxed a little. I went on with my speech, talking a little bit about how I got into the field in the first place, what I loved about it, why it excited me.

"The truth is, I love everything to do with the human body. I love working in the gym and seeing people push through their insecurities and preconceived notions to achieve things they never imagined possible. I love helping someone's body heal after an injury or overcome a new disability. Whether it's jogging alongside a client, instructing a client in the proper way to do the breaststroke, or just sitting down and chatting about nutrition and meal planning, my job gives me such a strong sense of fulfillment. I cannot imagine a life in which I don't do this. It's what I was born for, I think," I proclaimed.

I paused for a moment to shuffle my papers around. I glanced at Tyler again, and he gave me a very subtle thumbs-up. I stifled a laugh and went on.

"What originally sparked my interest in personal training as well as physical therapy and exercise medicine was when I joined the football team in high school. Believe it or not, my parents had me pegged as an academic back then," I said. A titter of laughter went through the room, just as I'd hoped. "They wanted me to try out for the speech and debate team, but I hated public speaking so much—no offense, Dr. Stone—that I decided to try out for football instead. And wouldn't you know it, I turned out to be pretty darn good at it. But it wasn't just the raw athleticism or game politics I was pulled into. What really made the football team an extraordinary part of my life was the team itself: the camaraderie, the teamwork, the synergy we all felt among ourselves. Whether it was running drills on the field at practice, scoring that magnificent final goal in the last milliseconds of a game, or just hanging out chatting and laughing in the locker room afterward, it was all a beautiful new world to me, one I was overjoyed to be a part of. I loved feeling that adrenaline pumping through my veins. I loved feeling like I was a part of something greater than me. And learning how to train my body to do things I could never do before... that inspired me deeply."

I stopped for a moment and moved my papers around again,

taking the opportunity to steal a glance over at Dr. Stone. To my relief, she was smiling placidly, just waiting for me to go on.

So I did.

"Another inspirational figure in my life was my football coach. He was the most patient, hard-working, dedicated coach I had ever seen. He treated the team almost more like family than just a sports team. He took us all under his wing individually, devising exercise and training regimens tailored to each of our respective needs. He could get a little hotheaded during tense games, of course, but never at us. He protected us. He worked hard for us. And it's partly his influence that has brought me to this classroom tonight," I explained, trying not to get choked up.

Having Tyler here was making me a little emotional, since he was part of the team back in the day, and I knew he knew exactly what I was talking about. I looked over at him, and he was gazing at me with so much love and respect it nearly made me buckle at the knees. But I remained strong. I had to at least make it through to the end of this presentation. And it was time for me to talk about him. I hoped I could manage to hold it together.

"But more recently, there's another person who has inspired me and reminded me that I know for certain this is the path I wish to follow. I have been working closely with a... a friend of mine who needed some guidance in getting back in shape. We put together a functional exercise and diet regimen that has given us clear and positive results. Standing alongside him as we push past boundaries and reach new heights has been incredibly rewarding. Watching him regain his confidence has been a treat for me, and it's reinforced my belief that this is my calling. This is what I want to do with my life. And I am so proud and elated to have gotten the opportunity to take this class and move forward with my career. I am so excited about the future, and I can't wait to get started. Thank you, everyone. Thank you, Dr. Stone," I concluded.

I returned to my seat amid a hail of applause, including from Dr. Stone, who was grinning from ear to ear. That was a good sign, for sure. As soon as I sat down, Tyler took my hand and gave it a tight squeeze.

"You did amazingly!" he gushed in an undertone.

"Only because you were here," I whispered. "Thank you."

"Of course. Anytime," he replied, eyes shining.

The remainder of my classmates went up to do their presentations, and then class ended early, giving Tyler and me just enough time to have a friendly chat with Dr. Stone before heading out. I introduced Tyler to her eagerly. Proudly.

"Oh, this is the client you talked about in your presentation?" she said.

I nodded. "Yes, ma'am. He's the one."

She smiled. "Nice to meet you, Tyler. Sounds like you two have a great working relationship. You're lucky to have each other," she said sagely.

"I agree," Tyler and I said at once.

We all laughed and said our goodbyes, Tyler and I heading out into the brisk spring evening. He looped his arm through mine as we walked across the quiet, darkened campus. There weren't a lot of courses that ran this late, so it felt eerily like we were alone here. But with Tyler by my side, it wasn't so much creepy as just, well, a little romantic. Every moment of alone time I got to spend with him felt that way. We walked in mostly silence, comfortable enough not to need to be chattering away constantly. We strolled slowly back to his car and got inside, immediately turning on the heat as we sat there. I could feel a sort of tension welling up between us, some unspoken worries and wishes that needed to be addressed. With some old country song playing ever so faintly on the car stereo, Tyler looked over at me. His face was half shadowed, half illuminated by the milky white lights of the campus parking lot. I followed the smooth lines of his face, the softness of his lips, the intensity in those gorgeous eyes. He was beautiful, from head to toe, and I longed to reach out and touch him, but I knew we had some stuff to talk about first.

"So," he began cautiously. "There's somethin' I've been meaning to talk to you about."

"Okay. Go ahead," I urged him softly.

"Well, first of all, I'm still worried about the game," he admitted with a heavy sigh. "I just don't know if I can swing it."

I frowned. "But you've made such great progress," I pointed out.

"But what if it's not enough? I mean, Bill and Jared are assholes, but what if they had a point? Losing weight hasn't magically turned me back into a nimble, athletic high school footballer who can take a hit. What if I can't do as well as I want to? What if I let the whole team down?" he rambled, looking worried.

I laid a hand on his shoulder. "Hey. Don't think that way. You've made great strides and not just weight-related. You're stronger now. Faster. More disciplined. You're prepared for this. I promise. Besides, it's just a game at the end of the day. It doesn't have to be the end-all, be-all proof of your success, Tyler," I explained.

"And second of all, there's something else I wanted to tell you," he said, sounding a little nervous. He sat up straighter and closed his eyes, taking a deep breath. My heart began to race as he opened his eyes and gazed at me adoringly.

"What is it?" I prompted softly.

"I don't want us to stop working together," he confessed with a sigh. "These weeks I've spent with you have been some of the happiest times of my life, Mace. I go to bed smiling, and I wake up smiling. Whenever you're near me, all I can feel is pure joy. And when we're apart, I just spend the whole time daydreaming about the moment we get to be together again. You've changed my life and my outlook in so many ways I could never even put into words. You've built me back up from scratch. You've given me strength where I thought I had none. You make me strong and confident and proud in a way I've never experienced before. And I know this big game is supposed to mark the end of our Plan, but... but I don't want it to. I don't want to let you go yet, Mason. Not now, not ever."

I stared at him in complete awe, my jaw dropped. This was certainly not the conversation I had expected to have tonight. But Tyler looked at me so pleadingly, with such longing. I knew he needed me to tell him how I was feeling. Which meant I would have to fully work out how I felt and put it into words that made sense.

Yikes.

"Well, what do you think?" he asked nervously.

"I think," I began slowly, "you have a damn good point."

"I do?" he asked, brightening up a little.

"Yeah, Ty. You and I make a great team. Working with you has been the single most rewarding thing I've ever done. All I ever want is to be with you. All the time. I can't get you out of my head, no matter how hard I try to pretend it's not happening. But it is happening. I'm falling in love with you, and I don't know what that means for us in the future. But it's something you need to know," I confessed. I felt lighter, as though a physical weight had actually been lifted off my shoulders.

Tyler beamed at me. "I'm falling for you, too," he said softly.

"Good. Good to know," I said with a laugh, leaning in to cup his face and kiss him on the lips.

He moaned against my mouth, and we both wriggled closer, kissing and holding one another in the faint light of the parking lot and the full moon hanging high above. There was no one left around here, nobody to see or hear us. We were alone together in his car, and we could no longer hold in the powerful feelings inside us. We ripped off each other's clothes and kissed every inch of one another's bodies. We caressed and stroked and groped and climbed into the back seat to better mold ourselves together as one. We rode our way higher and higher to the greatest heights of pleasure, wrapped up and enrobed in the warmth of authentic, undeniable passion. He was mine, and I was his, come what may.

TYLER

It had been a while since I held the red jersey that read *22* in bold white numbers, and I had to admit... I wore it well after all these years.

It was the day of the game, and I was in the locker room with the rest of the team getting into our uniforms. The chatter of the guys filled the room as we all checked each other out in our gear, laughing about the old times and who all they had seen so far. The reunion itself had been nothing to shout about if you asked me. Most of the people who showed up were cheerful enough to see each other, but half of us still lived in Winchester, so it hadn't taken long for us to break ourselves up into groups and spend a few hours sharing stories back and forth. Sure, it was nice to see a few familiar faces, but today, the main event was happening right here.

Mason had been at my side the whole time, and being able to introduce ourselves as boyfriends felt pretty damn good. It brought a few surprised faces, but each one was followed by a smile and a kind word. I liked showing Mason off, and I got the impression Mason liked showing me off as well, so we found a way to enjoy ourselves until the good stuff.

The game was taking place in the evening, just after sunset. Most of the reunion was over by now, except for some unofficial drinks that were taking place at the end of the night at The Chisel, courtesy of whichever team lost tonight. While I was the middle linebacker, Mason and Marshall were my 'Sam' and 'Will', meaning the linebackers who covered the sides of the offense with more and less guys on it, respectively.

"Lot of faces in the stands," Hunter said as he entered the locker room, taking his hat off. "Not just folks from the reunion, either."

"Of course not." Mason chuckled. "It wouldn't be Winchester if half the town didn't show up for a pickup game."

The team laughed, and we settled down as Hunter waved a hand, still grinning.

"All right, for all intents and purposes, this is a friendly pickup game," Hunter said. "No ref, just the honor system. We're all locals, so let's act like it. Everyone clear on what their job is? Good, because I ain't wasting my breath on a fancy speech. Let's hit the field."

Mason exchanged a look with me as the team gave a cheer, and I nodded to him before I put my helmet on, and we filed outside. I followed behind him, watching his ass for a moment before forcing myself to turn my eyes up to the old familiar floodlights that were greeting me as we stepped out onto the field.

Seeing the stands so full was far more jarring than watching the other team streaming out onto their side of the field. There were a lot of familiar faces in those stands, and all of them were giving cheers and applause as we came out. It was almost funny. Here we were, a bunch of men in our thirties, about to come out for a pickup game with our old comrades to see if we still had the mettle we had back in the day. It should have been the most low-pressure, friendly game we had ever tackled.

In reality, it was anything but that, especially for me.

Small towns like Winchester were thirsty for excitement, and that meant high school football was important to a lot of people. When a town wasn't big enough to have a college, a high school was often the biggest thing they had that could show off the kinds of people they raised and put them to the test. Football in Winchester and plenty of other rural towns like ours was a matter of local pride, not just the basic appeal of the sport. That went a long way, too. But for me, this was about proving to myself that I could pull my weight like I used to. I had seen an impressive change in myself over the past few weeks, and now, I had to get out there and prove myself... both to myself, and to Mason, no matter how much it didn't matter to him.

I couldn't help but think about Mason as we marched out. In my opinion, his reputation was far more important than mine. He was the quarterback, the guy who had gotten a scholarship to play college football, the one who could have been a player in the eye of national television. Yet he had preferred Winchester over that, and that had brought the two of us together. Despite all that, he carried himself as just Mason, a friendly face at the gym.

Tonight, I was fighting for his reputation as much as my own.

The other team eyed us as we gathered around for Hunter to lead the coin toss. He wasn't a referee or an official coach, but as the main organizer for the game, he was filling in all those roles in one way or another. As Hunter tossed the coin into the air, I locked eyes with Jared, who stood next to Bill, and he was smirking at me with a challenging bounce of his eyebrows. I gave him a stony glare in reply.

"Tails," Hunter declared, gesturing to Bill's team to indicate that they had been chosen to play offense.

That meant we were on defense, and *that* meant I was going to need to deliver right from kickoff. I felt a hand patting me on the shoulder, and I turned to see Mason nodding to me.

"Let's kick ass," he said, and I bumped my helmet against his in response before we jogged toward our end of the field, feeling more determined than ever.

We lined up at our end, and the football stood ready at the far end of the field as we stood poised, each one of us ready. Carter was our kicker, and when I glanced over to him, I saw Mason doing the same. The stands were quiet. Mark and his grandma Nancy Sullivan were among the faces gathered to watch us, as were Kate and Liz, even my parents. What looked like half the wives and children in Winchester were up there, and about as many other citizens looking on with proud smiles at all of us.

I felt a sense of peace just before the whistle blew.

Flawless was all I could think as I watched Carter approach the ball, legs working with perfect stride, and with enough force to break a brick, his foot hit the ball. It was the first kickoff I had been a part of in fifteen years, and the old rush came right back to me. The ball sailed high into the air as the offense maneuvered to catch it... and one of them did.

Jared caught the ball mid-sprint, and as the crowd cheered, he took off at top speed across the field, racing for our line. Immediately, every man on our team raced forward, myself included. There was exactly one thing we needed to do: get Jared on the ground and stop that ball from getting any further. I watched three of our linemen swarm him, and one of them went in for the tackle.

But he darted past him like a lightning bolt, and my eyes went wide. He had spotted an opening immediately, and he was taking it. Jared was a somewhat smaller guy by football standards, and that meant speed.

My every muscle sprang into action, and I raced for him. My feet pounded the ground as all of my frame sent me hurdling across the green toward Jared, who was moving so fast I realized that he and his group must have been training just as hard as we had been. I gained ground on him, so close on his tail that I could hear him breathing. Legs pushing me hard, I went in for the tackle... and Jared slipped out of my fingers.

I watched in disbelief as he darted through our entire line, and just before he reached the end zone, he turned to run sideways, holding his arms out and taunting us as he crossed the line, and half the stands cheered. There was no courtesy applause from our folks in the crowds. This was country football.

"Fuck," I murmured under my breath, and I looked back at the rest of the team.

Mason looked as stunned as I did, Marshall's face looked stormy through his helmet guard, and Carter was taking a deep breath. We had our work cut out for us, it seemed.

But by halftime, little had changed, and frustrations only ramped up. The opposing team had made their conversion, bringing the score to 7-0 in their favor. From there on out, it had been a relentless slog back and forth on the field, with neither team quite able to make much headway. That early touchdown had set the tone, against our favor, and that meant we had to pull it together if we thought we could make this work.

At 1st and 10 of the third quarter after a huddle, Mason was in his starring role as the quarterback, and I was his wide receiver, as I often did when playing offense in informal games. Poised in position, I waited for the sound of the snap, and I ran.

Everything was going as planned. Marshall and Carter utterly shut down the defense, and even though Bill was gaining on me, I was open. Mason sent the ball spiraling toward me. But before I could touch it, something else touched me.

Bill had raced up to me, and once he was in reach, he got just close enough that my body was between him and the rest of the team, and he stuck out an arm to shove me off balance.

I staggered, the ball hit the ground, and Bill caught it. That was a blatant offensive pass interference, a dirty trick that wasn't too uncommon but nevertheless illegal. I saw red. I was not about to let this asshole pull an underhanded stunt like that to steal Mason's thunder for what was about to be a solid play. Without a second thought, I lunged forward and tackled Bill to the ground with a satisfying *thud*.

"What the fuck, Bill?!" Mason barked as he stormed out toward us.

"I didn't do nothin'!" Bill protested as I got off him, and the team started to gather around. "My arm brushed him!"

"That was more than a brush," Mason snarled, and Marshall was approaching, looking like he was of the same mind.

"Hey, hey, hey," Rhett said, jogging forward from the other team. "We agreed to an honor system."

"Yeah, that only works if *you* stick to it too," Mason snapped.

"Tyler sure didn't think it was illegal when he tackled me," Bill pointed out, and Mason opened his mouth to retort, but he knew he was right.

Hell, so did I. From the looks on everyone's faces on our team, not a soul blamed me for tackling Bill, but that didn't change the fact that I had acted as if the ball were still in play.

"He's right," I admitted, shaking my head. "We play from here, where I laid Bill out on his face."

Begrudgingly, we started to line up, but Mason called a huddle. All of us gathered around while he delivered his plan. By the time we broke up and headed back to the line, I found myself thinking Mason was even crazier than I thought.

As soon as the ball touched Mason's hands, he backed up for a moment as if about to throw it to me, but I was not open. My job was to keep Bill occupied, just like everyone else on our team was keeping the other men occupied. Two seconds into the play, Mason bolted.

Having a quarterback run the ball was not something you did often in football, but Mason wanted to prove a point. And when that man of mine moved, he *moved*. While blocking Bill, I caught glimpses of his every muscle working in perfect harmony to carry him forward across the field while the crowd roared. The other team's tight end, a massive guy with biceps that an arm brace couldn't fit around, nearly took him down, but Mason leaped forward and kept just out of reach moments before crossing the line to the end zone. Although the crowd cheered along with the team, Mason didn't strut, flex, or taunt. He just tucked the ball under his arm, gave the other team a curt nod, and calmly jogged back to our team.

He gave me a high five, and I held on just long enough to get his attention and point from my eyes to his with a flirtatious smile. Mason winked in reply, and we got ready for the conversion. Carter's kick landed true, and just like that, the score was 7-7, tied.

And for almost another full two quarters, we stayed that way.

At 3rd and 7 in the last two minutes, while the offense's quarterback was huddled with his team calling a play, I was doing the same, and I decided it was time to change strategy. An MLB was a technical role to have, and it meant I had to play a similar role on defense to the offense's quarterback in that I strategized for us. That had always paired well with my mind for mechanics, and I hoped it would serve us well here...even though what I was about to call looked like anything but finesse on the surface.

"We're tied, and it doesn't look like we're going to get the chance to break that this game. But they are absolutely going to try for a field goal on the 4th down, so if we don't want that to happen, we need to push them back *yesterday*. This time, we're going to blitz," I said point blank as soon as we were in the huddle, and every set of eyes was locked on me. "That quarterback is way too comfortable, and we need the passer out of pocket. Marshall," I said decisively, pointing to the bouncer who looked like he could break a man in half, "put that QB on his ass, you hear me?"

"Don't have to tell me twice," he said with a ruthless grin.

"The rest of you, stay on where you've been and get that QB open," I ordered. "I want pressure on them for the 4th, and I want that ball in our hands by the end of it. Everyone good?"

"Hell yeah!" came the collective shout, and we broke up to take our places on the line of scrimmage.

I stepped back and readied myself in the silence that hung in that last few seconds before the hike. Right on cue, just a few seconds before the hike, I heard Marshall's heavy footsteps coming from behind me to my right, and they broke into a full-tilt sprint just as the offense snapped the ball to their quarterback.

But in those split seconds, I caught on to something.

The quarterback and I moved back at the same time, and I saw his eyes dart to his left. Following them, I saw a potential drag route coming my way—a wide receiver who was open and looking like he was about to get the ball passed to him in my territory. If this blitz worked, that pass would never happen, and the quarterback was going to get my freight train of a linebacker smashing into him.

Marshall *plowed* through two full grown men so hard that the audience winced at the sound of the crack of armor against armor. The quarterback's eyes went so wide that I thought he was about ready to piss himself at the sight of Marshall barreling toward him. But as he did, Mason rushed up on that receiver and had him on lock-down before I could blink. With Mason covering that, I drifted the opposite direction on a hunch. And that hunch proved right.

As I suspected, the quarterback's gaze snapped away from the drag run as Marshall closed the distance between them, that gaze went in my direction...because he was looking past me to Jared, who had darted behind me. This time, I was ready.

Fractions of a second before Marshall's body collided with his, the quarterback threw the ball toward Jared. The ball left his fingertips just before Marshall's whole force caught him and put him on the ground so hard I could have sworn it shook if I hadn't been jumping in the same instant.

My feet left the ground, and my body lurched into the air to inter-cept the ball as cleanly as a training video.

The sounds of cheering met me as I hit the ground again, and I took off running so hard I might as well have been flying. I shot cross-field diagonally, and my team kept the scrambling offense off me. My heart was racing, and adrenaline was working its magic like never before. All the adrenaline in the world wouldn't stop a strong tackle, though, and that was what I was faced as Bill charged me.

My mind almost went blank, and I did the only thing I had open to me. As my sprint carried me diagonally, I turned my shoulder just in time to smack Bill hard in the front and put him on his ass as my momentum kept me bounding forward. I felt a pair of hands slip around my waist, and I twisted away to avoid it. I had no idea my body could be that nimble, even after all the training Mason and I put ourselves through

The end zone was on me in a heartbeat, and I had to force myself to stop running to avoid galloping off the entire field. I turned and saw my team rushing toward me, and Mason was the first one to throw his arms around me. While the others gathered around, Mason pressed a kiss to my lips, neither of us caring that we were sweaty and grimy. My heart was soaring, but not as much as when I heard the first words out of Mason's mouth when he broke the kiss.

"I love you, Tyler!" he shouted over the cheering teammates.

"Fuck, I love you, man!" I laughed back, wrapping my arm around him and kissing him again.

With less than a minute left on the clock and their spirits broken, the other team didn't get that chance they'd been craving to score again. It was over. We had won, and in front of every friend, neighbor, and relative up there in the stands.

Mason and I did exactly what we came out here planning to do: we delivered.

Together.

MASON

"HELL YEAH, MAN! WE DID IT!" SHOUTED CARTER, RUNNING TO HIGH-five me. I laughed raucously and slapped his hand, hard, both of us grinning from ear to ear.

Mark came barreling down the field, slung over Tyler's shoulder and laughing hysterically. I almost buckled over at the ridiculous sight. Tyler gently rolled Mark down off his shoulders onto the green turf, all of us in impossibly high spirits.

"I can't believe it," Mark gasped. "I can't believe we won."

"I always knew we would," Carter said brightly. "A team like us? We're unstoppable!"

"You guys are all the best. I am so lucky to be surrounded by the most amazing teammates and friends a guy could ever have," Tyler gushed.

"Take that, assholes!" Mark hissed over his shoulder at the other team.

Luckily they were far enough away not to hear that comment. I looked back at them and nearly snorted with laughter when I saw how hunched over and beaten down they looked. I felt a tad bit guilty about how self-righteous we all were, but at the same time... those guys really were the pits. I generally tried to look at the world around me through a rosy lens of fairness and justice. I usually didn't let myself hold a grudge for very long. I have always just reminded myself that holding on to negative emotions was more likely to cause pain and suffering for me than to make me feel any better. But even I had to admit that tonight felt pretty damn good. Especially when I thought about the kind of rude comments those guys had made in the past, to Tyler most recently. They really did deserve to lose. And we had all worked our asses off to win.

But of course, I still had butterflies in my stomach. I had a feeling I knew what the end of this game signified for Tyler and me. After all, we had been working together all this time to prepare for the big game. It was always the event hovering on the horizon, just out of reach but swiftly approaching. Now that it had come and passed, I wondered what would become of the two of us? Would we shake hands and part ways, none the wiser? Would we pledge to stay friends and then drift apart as so many adult friendships do? Would we try to make it work and then fail?

Or, and this was the scenario that made my heart pound so hard it made me dizzy, what if we tried to make it work and… it worked? What if we could actually continue the way we had been for the past couple of weeks? What if this relationship, borne out of necessity, could fully blossom and bloom into something truly beautiful and real? There was no use pretending; I knew precisely what I wanted. And maybe there had been a time not so long ago when I would have guarded my heart against such a desire, when I would have shoved my feelings aside and kept everything professional and aboveboard. For so long, I had made my job the pinnacle and hinge-point of everything else. My life revolved around the gym, around my classes, on bettering myself so I could continue progressing in my career. I existed to help other people achieve their goals while simultaneously ignoring some of my own goals.

For example, I had kept myself so busy and preoccupied with work that I completely neglected to let myself fall in love. Until now. Until someone so amazing punctured through my fortress walls. Until Tyler managed to shift from old friend to client to lover. Now, I didn't want to picture my world without him in it. I needed him. He made me happy, and damn it, didn't I deserve to be happy, too?

Yes. It was time to confront what I felt. We had touched on it before, but I wanted to give it the full treatment this time. I needed to get Tyler alone. Today. Now.

I was shaken from my thoughts when Carter rushed over to pat me on the back, looking utterly exhilarated. "You comin' to The Chisel with us? We're planning to drink and eat nachos and celebrate the victory of the season!" he exclaimed.

I glanced over at Tyler, a silent question in my eyes. He met my gaze and gave a subtle, almost imperceptible nod. I turned back to Carter and smiled.

"Sure, yeah. We'll join you. But, uh, we have to make a stop first on the way," I said.

"All right, well, don't take too long! Join us when you're ready. We're going to be celebrating all night long, I bet," he said with a laugh.

Mark came up and slid an arm around his shoulders. "We'll see about that," he added with a wink. Then to me he said, "We'll meet you there."

"Perfect. Yeah, see you soon," I replied as Tyler fell into step beside me and the others rushed off, still whooping and fist-punching the air with excitement. Tyler and I shook our heads, laughing at their ridiculous antics.

"I can't believe it," Tyler murmured. "We really won."

"And you're the one who got us that victory, Ty. You're the hero," I told him.

He blushed adorably, and I draped an arm around his broad, thick shoulders, pulling him close. I kissed him on the cheek, which only made him blush harder. I couldn't stop staring at him. His smooth skin, the field lights reflecting like a fuzzy glow in his eyes, the way his cheeks ever so faintly dimpled when he smiled. He looked happy. Exhausted, but happy. I could feel the raw heat radiating off of his body from the exertion of the game. I knew for sure he had thrown his entire being into the game. He had really given it everything he had. We all did. And it had paid off in the end. God, what a satisfying feeling!

"There she is," I announced as we walked out to the old student parking lot. I gestured grandly to my truck. "Just as shiny and gorgeous as ever, thanks to you!"

Tyler chuckled. "I'm just so happy I could fix her. She's a real beauty. Would've been a big shame to lose seein' her out on the roads," he said.

"Couldn't agree with you more," I replied. "Come on inside. Let's get going."

We climbed into the truck, and I started driving, watching in the rearview mirror as our old high school shrank smaller and smaller behind us.

"It's odd," Tyler said suddenly in a curious voice. "That place used to be so intimidating to me, you know? And now it's like... it's like it's gotten so small. I wonder what I was ever afraid of to begin with."

"That's exactly how I feel. High school seems like a million years ago, yet there are parts of it I can recall like it was yesterday. I wonder if you ever fully forget what it was like to walk through those halls and play on that turf," I mused aloud.

"There are definitely some parts I wouldn't mind forgetting, but for the most part, it was all good," Tyler said pointedly.

I reached across the console to take his hand, and he gave it a light squeeze. I glanced over at him, and he was staring at me, those beautiful eyes luminous and full of questions. I swallowed hard, my stomach twisting nervously. This was going to be The Talk. But it didn't have to be difficult. In fact, I was pretty cool with the idea of making it as casual as possible. We both knew already what we needed to know.

"Listen, Ty," I began, heaving a deep breath. "I don't want to lose you."

"I don't want to lose you either," he said quickly, shaking his head.

"And I don't intend to," I said. "Hell, I would follow you anywhere, Tyler. I don't care. Don't get me wrong. I love my job. I love Winchester. I would love to stay here for the rest of my life and build a family here, settle in, live a quiet and happy existence. But if you told me you wanted to uproot and move to Siberia, I'd be right there behind you."

A warm, comforting smile spread across his handsome face.

"Well, lucky for you I have no interest in Siberia." He chuckled softly.

"You know what I mean," I said with a grin.

"I do. I do know," he answered in a quiet voice. "And you know what? I feel the same way, Mace. There's not another soul on earth who could have gotten me to jog and swim laps and lift weights and follow a diet. And there's definitely no one else who could make it so fun and easy as you do. I thought it was just an easy regimen, but I've realized it's actually pretty hard. It's just that everything comes so easily to me when I'm with you. Mason, you make me feel so confident and strong. I feel like I can do literally anything as long as you're beside me. I don't want to lose that feeling. I want to keep it and hold on to it for however long you will let me. I'm all in, Mason. Heart and soul."

I bit the inside of my cheek to keep the happy tears from burning in my eyes. I pulled the truck over and down a little-known rough trail, driving just several yards from the road, shaded and camouflaged by the dense trees. I stopped the truck and turned to give Tyler my full attention. I took both of his hands in mine, trying not to shake.

"There is no one else I would rather be with," I told him fervently. "You have made my world so bright and happy. Before I had you in my life, whenever I thought about the future, it just stressed me out, made me nervous. I didn't know exactly where I would end up. I mean, I assumed I would stay here in Winchester, but I always pictured myself alone. Not anymore. Now, all I want is you, Tyler. I just want to rise up and meet that future with you. We make such a great team. We'd be totally unstoppable together. I'm yours if you'll have me, Tyler. I promise you that."

"Thank goodness," he sighed, reaching to kiss me.

His lips were so soft and sensual against mine, and I immediately felt my body heating up. An idea suddenly occurred to me, and I broke apart. I reached into the back seat and grabbed a go-bag I kept packed for emergencies. Tyler watched with a quizzical expression as I pulled out a modestly sized fleece blanket, a tiny bottle of lube, and a pack of condoms. I looked up to see the blush creeping across Tyler's face, and I laughed gently.

"We could do it right here, you know," I said. "We don't have to if you don't –"

"I do," he said quickly. "I do."

I grinned, my heart racing like crazy. "Then let's do it."

We both hopped out of the truck cabin and rushed around back to the flatbed of my truck. I stretched out the blanket as we hurriedly pulled off our sweaty clothes. We collapsed onto the blanket together and fell into each other's arms, kissing and rocking against one another in perfect, needy rhythm. Our hands roved up and down each other's hard, sore bodies. We were both exhilarated and exhausted from the game, but we had just enough energy and passion left for this. In fact, with every kiss and every brush of his hand on my body, I felt that energy building. Tyler thrilled me all the way down to my core, and I was desperate to be close, as close as humanly possible.

He reached down and stroked my cock in his hand while he rutted his shaft against my leg. Meanwhile, I ripped open a condom wrapper and slid one on, then squirted some lubricant onto my fingers and began gently teasing the tight band of muscles around his entrance. Tyler groaned and closed his eyes, rutting to the rhythm of my fingers, moving against me wantonly. I kissed along his jaw and neck, breathing softly at the shell of his ear until he was keening and begging for more. I rolled my hips, his cock and mine sliding up against each other with delicious friction while I slipped one, then two fingers inside him. He gasped and clung to me tightly, his face flushing pink as I worked him open.

"God, I want you so badly," I hissed.

"You're all I ever think about these days," he choked out between gasps of pleasure. "You're everything I've ever wanted, Mason."

"And you are everything to me," I replied, kissing him on the lips again.

"Please," he murmured against my lips. "Fuck me. Take me. I'm yours."

"Turn around," I whispered.

He followed my command and turned to face away from me. I wrapped my arms around him, essentially spooning his body as I guided the head of my cock to his tight ass. I began to slowly push inside while Tyler trembled and groaned, panting in my arms. I was cautious, not wanting to hurt him, but he was desperate for it. He rocked back against me, both of us moving in slow tandem until I was fully sheathed inside him, feeling his tightness clench and squeeze around my engorged shaft. I kissed the back of his neck, and goose bumps prickled up on his skin as we began to rock back and forth. I reached around to stroke his cock while I fucked him from behind under the soft moonlight and the scattering of bright stars.

"I adore you," I murmured into his ear. "I adore you completely."

"And I love you so much I can barely stand it," Tyler choked out, twitching slightly in my arms at the intense onslaught of pleasure.

Slowly but passionately, we moved against and within one another in the flatbed of my beloved truck, warming each other's bodies with closeness and cradling one another as we ratcheted higher and higher to the peaks of bliss. Finally, with one last shudder, we came together. Tyler's cock spurted hot, slick spunk all over my fingers while my own cock convulsed and released inside him. We moaned and clung to each other through the aftershocks of bliss, too overstimulated and comfortable to move at first. Then, once we came down from the high, I kissed the back of his neck and gave him a tight hug before withdrawing. We cleaned ourselves up with the blanket and methodically put our clothes back on, both of us wearing similar grins.

As we got back in the truck and drove to The Chisel, I looked over at Tyler and laid a hand on his thigh. "You know, I don't think I've ever been this happy before in my life," I remarked.

Tyler took my hand and lifted it to his lips to kiss it gingerly.

"Same here. I'm just in awe of how happy I feel. It's all your doing, you know," he said, eyes shining with passion.

"Good. Because I intend on spending every day from here on out doing everything I can to keep you happy," I declared.

"And I will do the same for you," Tyler agreed. "I love you, Mace."

I grinned, feeling like my heart might burst out of my chest.

"I love you too, Ty," I told him, starting to get choked up.

But we both managed to hold it together, and when we walked into The Chisel hand in hand, we were greeted by a raucous group of happy teammates. We sat in the bar and drank and laughed for hours, neither of us wanting to be anywhere else but there. Together. As it should be.

THE END

WEIGHT FOR LOVE (WORTH THE WEIGHT BOOK 1)

If you enjoyed *Hard Tackle (Worth the Weight Book 2)*, you'll enjoy *Weight for Love (Worth the Weight Book 1)*. These books are connected within the same world, but they can be read as standalone novels.

Description:

<u>MARK:</u>

Two things are off the menu: straight men and delicious food.

As luck would have it, those are the first temptations I encounter when I return to my hometown to help renovate the family house. It turns out that Winchester has a warm welcome for me, and his name is Carter.

But thinking about love would be a lot easier if I weren't so worried about my weight.

My homecoming starts with a broken-down car just as I arrive, and of course Carter is the first person to drive by. He's even fitter and sexier than when I left. I thought those piercing eyes were only for the ladies, but I was wrong. Oh so wrong. We want each other, but I'm not sure if I deserve a guy like Carter.

Maybe it's time to show him what my body can really do.

I might be cutting calories, but Carter's one indulgence I can't refuse.

CARTER:

Mark thinks he needs to slim down, but I'd rather see him strip down.

I missed my chance in high school, and I never thought I'd see Mark again. But he's back in town and looking better than ever. When I give his car a jump, sparks fly, and he's even more charming than I remember.

Luckily, I'm the contractor renovating his grandma's house, which means we'll be seeing a lot of each other. I don't care about labels. I want Mark, and I can't hide my excitement.

He's the one who got away. I want to give him the romance we missed out on in high school. But Mark is holding back. I like him at any weight, but he's determined to change himself. His dedication makes me hot, but I want him to know that I find him sexy no matter what.

Mark says he wants a workout partner, and I hope clothing is optional.

This is the first book in the Worth the Weight series. It can be enjoyed as a standalone with no cliffhanger. Readers can expect a steamy MM romance with several scenes that will leave you gasping. Heat level: 10.

ALSO BY JASON COLLINS

Worth the Weight Series:

Weight for Love (Worth the Weight Book 1)

Hard Tackle (Worth the Weight Book 2)

Standalone Novels:

His Submissive

Protecting the Billionaire

The Weight is Over

The Boyfriend Contract

Chasing Heat

Dom

Weight for Happiness

Straight by Day

Raising Rachel

The Warehouse

The Jewel of Colorado

Love & Lust

Forbidden

55329943R00112

Made in the USA
Columbia, SC
12 April 2019